KONOSUBA
GOD'S
BLESSING 10
ON THIS
WONDERFUL
WORLD!

Gamble
Scramble!

"Elroad?
Did you say
Elroad? As
in, Elroad,
the Casino
Kingdom?"

Aqua

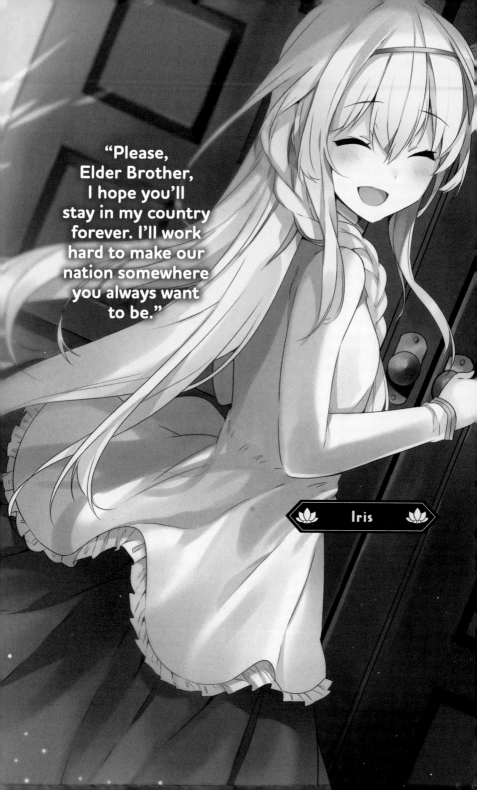

"Please,
Elder Brother,
I hope you'll
stay in my country
forever. I'll work
hard to make our
nation somewhere
you always want
to be."

Iris

KONOSUBA: GOD'S BLESSING ON THIS WONDERFUL WORLD! 10

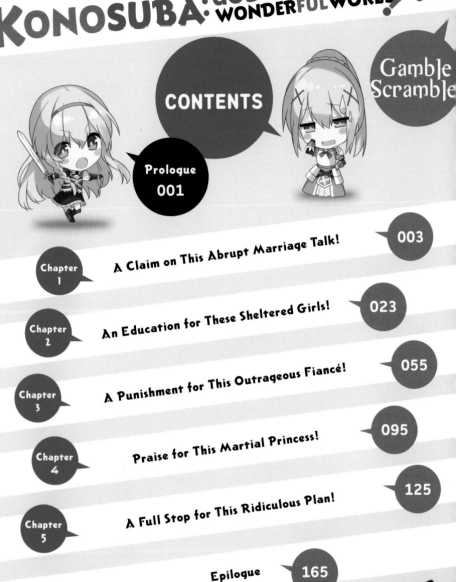

Gamble Scramble

CONTENTS

Illustrations/Kurone Mishima
Design/Yuko Yaoya +
Nanafushi Nakamura
(Mushikago Graphics)

KONOSUBA: GOD'S BLESSING ON THIS WONDERFUL WORLD!

Gamble Scramble!

10

NATSUME AKATSUKI

ILLUSTRATION BY
KURONE MISHIMA

YEN ON
NEW YORK

KONOSUBA: GOD'S BLESSING ON THIS WONDERFUL WORLD! 10

NATSUME AKATSUKI

Translation by Kevin Steinbach
Cover art by Kurone Mishima

KONO SUBARASHII SEKAI NI SHUKUFUKU WO!, Volume 10: GYANBURU SUKURANBURU!
Copyright © 2016 Natsume Akatsuki, Kurone Mishima
First published in Japan in 2016 by KADOKAWA CORPORATION, Tokyo.
English translation rights arranged with KADOKAWA CORPORATION, Tokyo, through TUTTLE-MORI AGENCY, INC., Tokyo.

English translation © 2019 by Yen Press, LLC

Yen On
150 West 30th Street, 19th Floor
New York, NY 10001

Visit us at yenpress.com
facebook.com/yenpress
twitter.com/yenpress
yenpress.tumblr.com
instagram.com/yenpress

First Yen On Edition: December 2019

Yen On is an imprint of Yen Press, LLC.
The Yen On name and logo are trademarks of Yen Press, LLC.

Library of Congress Cataloging-in-Publication Data
Names: Akatsuki, Natsume, author. | Mishima, Kurone, 1991– illustrator. | Steinbach, Kevin, translator.
Title: Konosuba, God's blessing on this wonderful world! / Natsume Akatsuki ; illustration by Kurone Mishima ; translation by Kevin Steinbach.
Other titles: Kono subarashi sekai ni shukufuku wo. English
Description: First Yen On edition. | New York, NY : Yen On, 2017–
Identifiers: LCCN 2016052009 | ISBN 9780316553377 (v. 1 : paperback) |
ISBN 9780316468701 (v. 2 : paperback) | ISBN 9780316468732 (v. 3 : paperback) |
ISBN 9780316468763 (v. 4 : paperback) | ISBN 9780316468787 (v. 5 : paperback) |
ISBN 9780316468800 (v. 6 : paperback) | ISBN 9780316468824 (v. 7 : paperback) |
ISBN 9780316468855 (v. 8 : paperback) | ISBN 9781975385033 (v. 9 : paperback) |
ISBN 9781975332341 (v. 10 : paperback)
Subjects: CYAC: Fantasy. | Future life—Fiction. | Adventure and adventurers—Fiction. |
BISAC: FICTION / Fantasy / General.
Classification: LCC PZ7.1.A38 Ko 2017 | DDC [Fic]—dc23
LC record available at https://lccn.loc.gov/2016052009

ISBNs: 978-1-9753-3234-1 (paperback)
978-1-9753-3235-8 (ebook)

10 9 8 7 6 5 4 3 2 1

LSC-C

Printed in the United States of America

KONOSUBA: GOD'S BLESSING ON THIS WONDERFUL WORLD!

Gamble Scramble!

Characters

Aqua

Job ▶ Arch-priest

An untamable goddess of water. Specialty: party tricks.

Kazuma Satou

Job ▶ Adventurer

Our NEET protagonist. His Luck is his only decent trait.

Darkness

Job ▶ Crusader

A tanky knight with a major masochistic streak. Daughter of an influential noble house.

Megumin

Job ▶ Arch-wizard

Genius of the Crimson Magic Clan. Not interested in anything except explosion magic.

Chomu-suke

A black cat and Megumin's familiar.

Emperor Zel

Aqua's pet chick.

Iris

First princess of the kingdom of Belzerg. Adores Kazuma like a brother.

I felt a gentle vibration against my back. Iris was still fawning over her ring.

"Hey. I know I keep saying this, but that's a cheap toy. It only cost four hundred eris. When we get back to the capital, I can get you a way better one."

"You don't have to! I don't need another ring. I like this one!"

It was the umpteenth time she had told me that.

"Yeesh, what's gotten into you today? Are you showing that off to me? Are you that eager for it to be snatched away?"

"Wh-what's wrong with you?! Do you wish to throw down?!"

It was also the umpteenth time Megumin had tried to steal Iris's ring.

We were in a cramped lizard carriage. As Megumin made a swipe for the ring, I said, "Keep your pants on. I bought you some Elroad rice crackers, didn't I? Even they cost more than that ring."

"It isn't a question of price! Yes, those rice crackers were delicious, yet somehow I feel like I received the short end of the stick here!"

Iris slipped her ring onto her finger to keep it away from the surprisingly sore Megumin. "I'm Elder Brother's little sister. And little sisters are special. Even more special than friends!"

"Ooh, what's that? Why have I been demoted to Kazuma's friend?! I am his adventuring companion and housemate! That makes me more than friends and less than family!"

I could hear someone napping peacefully in the carriage's rear.

"Well, I'm his little sister, so that makes me family. Which makes me above you, Miss Megumin!"

"That does it! You've been spoiling for a fight with me all day, and now you've got one!"

Yeah, the two of them were pretty loud.

"The royal family is strong! I will not, absolutely *will not* lose!!"

But I decided to take a nap myself.

Chapter 1

A Claim on This Abrupt Marriage Talk!

1

The Dark God Wolbach, general of the Demon King's army. One of the kingdom's most wanted, a villain who had harassed the capital's elite troops with powerful explosion magic despite the fact that some of her power was still sealed away.

The Demon King's general *and* a possible goddess? Whatever. We took her out and proved that our party was the real deal and not just a bunch of lucky idiots.

And now that we had led a group of top-tier adventurers to victory against the Demon King's army and our fame had started to spread far and wide...

"I think we should go capture a wild Dullahan."

"I have no idea what you're talking about."

I was lounging on a sofa in the mansion while Megumin watched in concern.

"What's with you, Kazuma? Have you spontaneously come to believe in the Axis Church and developed a desire to exterminate the undead? Well, I think that's wonderful, but you don't see wild Dullahans every day. You'll have to make do with skeletons and ghosts for a while."

I turned to the eternally out-of-it Aqua and launched into an explanation of *why* I wanted to capture a wild Dullahan. "I want to get my hands on one of those so I can learn the Herald Death skill. I really need it for a plan I've got in mind. Do you know if there's, like, a Dullahan spawn point around here anywhere?"

"Huh?! First it's Drain Touch, a *Lich* ability, and now this! What is your obsession with disgusting, filthy skills? Hand over your Adventurer's Card! I'm putting all your skill points into good, clean party-trick abilities like mine!"

"Hey, knock it off, you idiot! You can't do that! At least give me your healing magic or something!"

I shoved Aqua away as she tried to grab my Adventurer's Card. Darkness, sitting on the couch with Chomusuke on her knees, eyed me suspiciously. The little fur ball had gotten meaner and meaner toward Aqua ever since our last trip, looking for any opportunity to bite at her feather mantle. In other words, she was turning into a cat with attitude.

"Why *do* you want to learn a nasty skill like that? You know Dullahans rank right below vampires and Liches when it comes to undead, don't you? They don't show up out of the blue."

I was disappointed to hear that. In a world where Liches ran small-town shops with demons for assistants, I wouldn't have been surprised to find a Dullahan working in a haunted house somewhere.

Megumin, picking up on my reaction, asked nervously, "What do you have in mind? If you want a skill that powerful, Kazuma, you must be thinking of fighting an awfully serious enemy. Can I help you somehow? Can my Explosion, which has buried so many generals of the Demon King, not be of use?"

I tried to smile, not wanting to worry my companions, who were so eager to help. "No, that's not it. Thanks, Megumin. I'm sure your Explosion will help. You're right—no use pining after something I can't have... All right, Megumin, you and I are going to the next country over! We'll drop an explosion on the neighboring capital, then send 'em a letter: *If you don't want to suffer from any more explosions, break off the engagement with Princess Iris. We, the Demon King's army, will never recognize the marriage—*"

"Have you lost your mind?! I thought you'd been acting strange ever since you got that letter from Lady Iris... Is *this* what you've been plotting?! You wanted Herald Death so you could curse Lady Iris's betrothed, didn't you?! Why would the Demon King's army even care about that?!"

Darkness was not happy with my perfect plan.

"How dare you insult me like that! Yes, I was hoping to put a curse on Iris's future husband or whatever. 'Huh?!' they would say. 'This is definitely the work of the Demon King. Capturing princesses is his job, after all. He didn't want anyone horning in on his racket. We have highly skilled Arch-priests here, so we can remove the curse, but he might simply get cursed again. Until the Demon King is defeated, the only thing to do is to break off the engag—'"

"Despicable! This man is the worst! You want to use precious skill points for a low-down dirty thing like that? You should be ashamed!"

Now Megumin was piling on, too.

"I know Cooking, I know Flee, and *now* you complain about the kinds of skills I'm learning? I even learned the Read Lips skill recently so I could find out if adventurers at the Guild were talking about me behind my back."

"Y-you really have given up all pretense of adventuring. At least don't drag Megumin into your ridiculous plans."

I was being lectured by one person who knew only Explosion and another who had put all her skill points into defense. They didn't have any right to talk. I wanted to tell them to learn a few useful skills themselves before offering criticism.

...Weirdly enough, the only one who didn't seem to get drawn into this discussion was Aqua. "I'd be happy to be a part of that plan," she said finally. "I like the part where we blame the Demon King for everything. Smearing the Demon King's name is considered to be one of the obligations of members of the Axis Church, after all."

"Don't tell me you Axis people are the reason the Demon King has it out for humanity."

I really did have a reason for bringing this up all of a sudden.

I had gotten a letter from Iris just the other day. In it, she had asked me to be her bodyguard on a trip to a neighboring country to meet her future husband for the first time. Seeing as I'm basically her adoptive brother, I couldn't say no to anything my little sister wanted. I had recently been making preparations for the trip, like sharpening my sword (which I hadn't been caring for at all) so I could take on any good-for-nothing who thought he was going to get his hands on my adorable little sister.

"Okay, fine, we'll take the legal route. We agree to be her bodyguards, then interfere every chance we get. This could be a great opportunity to use up some of the skill points I've got lying around—if I can get someone to teach me a useful skill…"

At that point, I was busy muttering to myself and hadn't noticed. Darkness was looking at me, deeply disturbed.

2

The day after all this happened.

"Hey. Mind telling me just what the hell's going on?"

When I woke up a bit past noon, I found myself tied up helplessly on my bed for some reason.

"Ah, Kazuma, you're awake. Sorry, but for the next few days, I'm going to have to keep you tied up. Don't worry—I'll bring you the richest food I can find, and I'll help tend to all your needs. If there's anything you want, I'll send a servant to get it posthaste."

I didn't know when Darkness had gotten into my room, but she was looking at me triumphantly and firing up the crazy train first thing in the morning.

I didn't think she could have gone crazy from the heat. Summer was almost over.

"Did that screw in your head finally come loose? What's the big idea tying me up? *You're* the one who's into that, not me. Are you so madly in love with me that you couldn't hold yourself back anymore?"

"I am so *not* in love with an arrogant loudmouth like you! And don't talk about who likes what. This has nothing to do with my preferences." She glared down at me where I lay on the bed.

"You're such a pain. You kissed me and stuff—even if it was on the cheek—and now you're not into me all of a sudden? The *tundere* act is really getting old, y'know."

"I beg your pardon?! Look, that has nothing to do with this. And to think, after we had such a nice moment, I saw you chatting with one person and flirting with... Never mind—now isn't the time. We need to talk about Lady Iris." Apparently ready to move past her tongue-lashing, Darkness cleared her throat. "I'm sorry, Kazuma. Regarding the body-guard request Lady Iris sent us, I've taken the liberty of writing a letter of refusal. She'll be leaving in three days, so until I'm sure she's safely on her way, it's the ropes for you. Just take it easy until then."

She truly did look a little apologetic...

"Oh, you gotta be— Is *that* what this is about?! If we don't do something, my little sister is gonna be married off to some rando!"

"Says a commoner from gods-know-where! If you're any better than any other wanderer, then tell me about your background already! ...You know, I've always wanted to ask you. What country *do* you come from? Why do you sometimes display such unusual knowledge? And why do you so frequently lack the basic manners and common sense of an ordinary human be—?!"

"Megumiiin! Aquaaaa! Save me—our perv-sader can't even wait till after lunch to tie me up!"

"H-hey, you, don't make it sound so weird! And I'm sorry to tell you this, but Aqua and Megumin happen to be out of the house right now. All that's left is to summon a servant from my own home and have you transported, bed and all, to my mansion. If we let you guard Lady Iris, I can only imagine the diplomatic problems you'd cause. This is in the best interest of our country, so just bear with it."

"I wouldn't cause 'diplomatic problems'! I learned how to act like a noble back when I was living in the castle, and I wouldn't be rude, so let me go!"

"Rudeness is like second nature to you!" Darkness crouched down to look me in the eye, like she was talking to a child throwing a tantrum.

"If you sit quietly, I'll feed you some delicious delicacies. You're a simple layabout NEET anyway, aren't you? What could be better than having an excuse to sleep all day and have someone else take care of you?"

I suddenly realized this wasn't the time. "…Yeah, you're right about that. Okay, I understand."

"Y-you do…?! There's been so much working and fighting recently, a few quiet days with you would be really—"

—*nice*, I think she was about to say, shy smile on her face and everything, but I immediately broke in:

"Right, then, I've been desperate to go to the bathroom ever since I woke up. Hurry up and do something about it."

Blunt and to the point.

"…Huh?"

"Don't 'huh' me. Didn't you say you'd take care of all my needs? I assume you meant *all* my needs."

"………*Huh?*"

Darkness merely stood there, frozen.

"So consider this my first order. Darkness, help me pee."

"Whaaaaaa—?!"

"Don't 'whaaaaaa' me—just do it. Talk about your worthless noblewomen. I'm just asking you to keep your word. Hop to it already."

This was *not* sexual harassment. I could hardly move a muscle, so what else was I supposed to do?

Yep. I was totally in the right.

"Wh-wh-whoa! That's not what I meant! That is, Kazuma, I did say I would see to your needs, but not like tha— Wait a moment!"

"How am I supposed to wait? I woke up, and now I need to pee. It's practically a law of nature. And just so you know, this is how it's going to be every day from now on, got it? I don't want some weirdo servant from your house who I've never met manhandling me. So hurry up."

"Urrrgh… B-but…" Darkness was reduced to a gibbering wreck.

"C'mon—this isn't funny anymore. How much time are you gonna waste being embarrassed? I helped *you* go to the bathroom, remember? I helped you pull down your pants, and I even helped you reach the toilet paper. We've known each other too long to get all flustered over something like this. Hurry up and untie me. Just the bottom is fine."

I could feel the pee coming, and I was getting desperate.

Darkness, though, said in a small voice, "...I can't."

"...Wh-what?" I sputtered.

Darkness looked down apologetically. "I wasn't thinking about having to help with...*that* stuff. Wh-what am I gonna do? I used a really powerful magical item to bind you, and the binding can't be undone until it wears off. You're stuck for the next three days..."

"You moron! What am I supposed to do, lie here for three days?! You gotta be kidding me! I swear I'll make you suffer the same fate!"

Darkness turned red and fidgety under my verbal assault. "The s-same fate...?"

"Don't get all excited; this is an emergency! Gah, dammit!"

I raised my head—the only thing I could move—and took stock of my situation. It looked like I had been subjected to some form of Bind; ropes made of an almost rubbery material ran from my shoulders to my knees. They didn't look very strong, but if the item really was that powerful, then it was probably no use trying to break free of my bonds.

I might be able to barely slip out, though.

"Hey, Darkness, with your strength, you should be able to loosen a rope a tiny bit. Slide one of the ropes on my lower body aside just a little. Then you can pop me out and I can take it from there."

"A-all right, let me handle it!"

Still a bit red, Darkness got to work on the ropes. They were nice and tight, but I thought we could produce just enough of a gap to free my...you know.

"Okay, good work. I've got a pee bottle over there. Could you grab it for me?"

"......Why do you have something like that? Why in the world would you—?"

"A NEET's gotta do what a NEET's gotta do. You know how much of a pain it is to get up and go to the bathroom in the winter when it's freezing cold. That thing's a lifesaver."

"I—I had no idea you had sunk so low… Well, I will admit to its convenience in this scenario. I'll set it right here." With a look of disgust, Darkness placed the pee bottle in front of me…

"Hey, I can't go like this. I need you to pull down my pants and help me do my business."

"What?!"

How did she *think* this was going to work?

"Don't 'what' me—my hands are tied, and I can't move an inch. And you're the one who put me in this situation! Seriously, hurry up! The dam's gonna burst!"

"Y-y-yeah, but—! Oh, for…"

Darkness, on the verge of tears, looked away and reached out.

Then, with my pants halfway down, she made a strange face.

"Hmm…? Hey, Kazuma, your pants are stuck on something; I can't pull them down… Wait, is that…?"

"Sorry. Happens every morning. It's just biology."

………

"W-waaaaaaaaaaaahhhh!"

"Aaaaaagggh!! What are you doing?! Stop it! Stop! You're gonna rip it off!" I won't say exactly what *it* was, but I forgot all about amusing myself by harassing Darkness and gave a heartfelt scream. "What's wrong with you?! I almost did a class change on my sex! I swear, you remember this, 'cause I'm gonna make you *cry* when these ropes come off!"

"You're already making me cry… Hey, Kazuma, how about we give up on this? Come on—Aqua will be home soon, and we can have her use Create Water and Purification to clean everything up…"

"You're telling me to do it in my pants! You're telling me to just give up and pee myself! Stop being a moron and help me out! The reason you can't do it is because you're trying to look away, but you're the one who got us into this mess, so take some responsibility and *help me!*"

Darkness reached for my pants again, her eyes fixed firmly on my lower body this time. "Grrr, it wasn't supposed to be this way…! I just wanted to keep Lady Iris safe by ensuring you'd stay away from her… B-but now that I think about it, for a noblewoman like me to be forced to take care of someone's bathroom needs, to be ordered to look— maybe it's not so bad after all…"

"Listen, you idiot, quit flapping your gums and hurry! We're almost out of time! …Crap, I can't do it. I can't hold it any longer!"

"N-no, Kazuma, I'm taking care of it right now! Don't relieve yourself yet! Aaarrrgh, if Aqua or Megumin saw us now…!"

She didn't get to finish her sentence. I felt a pair of eyes on me from the door. I looked over to find Aqua peering through the half-open doorway like a housekeeper walking in on her employers.

"Woooooooow… I had no idea Darkness and Kazuma had gotten to the point where they were doing such dirty things together… I'm gonna go let everyone at the Guild know all about this!"

""Hold it right there!""

"Phew. You saved my neck, Aqua. Thanks to this perv, I almost peed myself."

Aqua's magic had broken the item's Bind. I went in the next room and relieved myself. Darkness was looking weepy and mumbling to herself, "Ohhh… 'P-perv…' 'Perv,' he called me…"

"That's nothing new, so I don't really care, but what kind of game were you playing?"

"A-Aqua?!"

Darkness seemed shocked for some reason, so I offered an explanation instead. "You remember how Iris asked us to do bodyguard work for her? And you remember how Darkness was really against it for some reason? Long story short: She tied me up and was planning to take me back to her house to do all sorts of naughty things to me until I missed my chance to leave for the quest."

"Darkness, how can you expect *not* to be called pervy when that was your plan?"

"I wasn't going to do anything naughty! …I really do think we could get into huge trouble this time, though. Lady Iris's betrothed is the first prince of Elroad, a neighboring kingdom. I hear he's really touchy, and if you guys pulled your usual tricks with him, it could end up being a diplomatic incident."

A prince with his head up his ass? All the more reason I had to protect Iris.

Aqua, meanwhile, got a gleam in her eye.

"Elroad? Did you say Elroad? As in, Elroad, the Casino Kingdom?"

I didn't recognize the name, but Aqua obviously did. A casino kingdom sounded like fun, though.

Now Aqua was fully on board. Darkness frowned and said, "Aqua, just to be clear, we'd be going as bodyguards, not to play around, okay? Hey, if you really want to go to Elroad that badly, let's make it our next vacation! We don't have to take a job to get there. We have plenty of money; we can enjoy ourselves!"

Despite Darkness's desperate attempt to dissuade her, it was clear from Aqua's face that she already had her heart set on going.

I nodded with satisfaction. "Cool, looks like Aqua agrees we should take this quest! When Megumin gets home, maybe we should put it to a vote. Not that I expect her to turn down the chance to go out on a quest!"

"Ugggghhhh……"

Darkness put her head in her hands. I smiled, confident I had her beat.

3

"Count me out."

That evening.

Megumin arrived riding on Yunyun's back—she must have been out for her daily Explosion—and managed to cough up an exhausted but resolute answer.

I didn't know why, but Megumin had turned into quite the contrarian ever since we got back from beating Wolbach. These days, she'd even started taking Yunyun on her "Explosion walks" instead of me.

"What do you mean, count you out? Normally I'd expect you to be all, *Is this some powerful opponent we haven't faced yet?* and hop right on board."

Megumin, settled deep into the sofa in our living room, quickly glanced at the kitchen, where Aqua and Darkness were making dinner, then looked back at me. "There is no *what* or *why* about it. This man! He wants every excuse not to move a muscle, but then someone mentions Iris, and suddenly he cannot wait to get involved."

Now she was baiting me, and I bit: "Ooh, is that jealousy I hear?"

But instead of getting angry like I expected—like she always did—Megumin just looked at me levelly. "Yes, I am jealous. After what happened between us, would it kill you to give me a little more attention?"

"Huh? …Oh, um, right." Confronted by Megumin's absolute seriousness, I found I was the one who felt my face getting hot.

When she said "what happened between us," she probably meant the night we nearly crossed the final frontier. But hang on a sec… Had Megumin ever been the type to say things like that? She seemed…less reserved, more assertive, like she wasn't willing to keep anything inside anymore.

"Does Iris really mean that much to you, Kazuma?" Megumin asked, still looking straight at me.

"Er, w-well, I kind of can't let her go. Not so much as a woman, y'know, but more like as a little sister who always has to ignore what she wants because of her position. She spends all her time worrying about everyone around her, so she must be kind of lonely."

I might have been a NEET, but I was no lolicon. Iris was nothing more than an adorable younger sister to me. Though I admit that in the future, if she grew up and said, *Big Bro, I wanna be your bride,* well, I wouldn't necessarily be against granting that wish.

Caught off guard by Megumin's attitude, I found myself talking a little too fast and worried that my face was turning red. "Anyway," I babbled on, "if you're really against it, Megumin, then I'll think of some other way. If we were to take on bodyguard duties, I would want us all to do it together anyway. I'll miss seeing Iris, but…"

"Let us accept, then," Megumin said shortly with a small sigh. "I'm concerned about that girl myself. This was nothing more than a passing fit of jealousy."

"Uh—sure!"

What was with this honest display of affection? My ears were burning hot. I was just thinking about casting Freeze on my own face (I couldn't believe a younger girl was leading me by the nose like this) when Darkness and Aqua emerged from the kitchen with dinner.

"Megumin, you're back," Darkness observed. "It's our treat tonight! …Kazuma, why is your face so red?"

"N-n-n-no special reason! Right, Megumin?"

Unlike me, deeply shaken to have had Darkness point out the color of my cheeks, Megumin smiled. How could she be so calm? She was making me look like a trembling idiot.

"Gosh, Megumin, if you'd come home sooner, you could have seen the funniest thing. Darkness had tied Kazuma to the bed and was trying to pull his pants down!"

"Oh-ho," Megumin said, surprised by Aqua's entirely unnecessary information.

"Stop that, Aqua—I wasn't doing anything naughty! Yes, I did tie him up, that's true, but like I explained—" Darkness, her hands full of dishes, kept stealing little glances at Megumin to see how she was reacting.

But me, I said: "Yeah, and if Aqua had gotten home a little later, Darkness actually would have pulled my pants down. She really saved me."

"Whaaaa—?!" Now the crimson of Megumin's eyes flashed. "…Well, whatever Darkness (who is constantly horny) does and whomever she does it with is no concern of mine. But still, I can hardly approve of the daughter of a good family forcibly making someone her prisoner!"

"Th-th-th-th-th-that's not—! Megumin, that's not what happened; I swear there was a reason for this! And don't call me 'constantly horny'!"

Darkness launched into a desperate attempt at an explanation, but the rest of us already had our eyes fixed on the dishes piled on the table.

"I wonder if you'll recognize what I've set out here, Kazuma," Aqua was saying. "I know how sharp your senses are from the food tours we've done. That's right: Tonight's dinner is blowfish! And not just any blowfish but the Paradise Blowfish, the king of them all. Its poison is a lot more powerful than any other blowfish, but true gourmands say that if they died eating this food, it would be worth it! And it happens to be in season right this moment."

"I don't know if the name describes the fish or where it sends you when you eat it. I'm impressed you know how to cook blowfish, though. I always took you for a party clown, but you do have a real skill or two."

Megumin and I took our seats, enamored by our dinner. Blowfish sashimi, blowfish stew, blowfish *chawanmushi*. There was a little plate of what looked like roe, along with a tiny cooking brazier filled with blowfish fins. It was enough to make you drool just from looking at it. I couldn't wait; I reached out...

"Of course I don't know how to cook blowfish. If you feel yourself going numb, let me know, and I'll use antidote magic on you."

"Hey."

And that, right there, was another loud reminder of how sketchy this world could be...

I had just put back the *chawanmushi* I'd picked up when I heard a slurping sound from beside me.

"Delicious!"

"Don't eat that; don't you know it might be poisonous?!"

Megumin had grabbed the dish I'd set down and was devouring it. In fact, before I knew it, Darkness, sitting across from me, had stabbed the blowfish sashimi with her fork and was shoving it into her mouth.

Geez, didn't these people ever hesitate?

They assumed blowfish and antidote magic went hand in hand. I guess in a world where magic was real, that made a certain kind of sense, but…

Darkness saw me watching her and grinned. No doubt looking for a little payback for earlier, she said, "What's wrong, Kazuma? Is our big, brave adventurer afraid of a little fish? Aqua's a superb priest, if nothing else, so what's there to worry about?"

"Uh, Darkness, did you say 'if nothing else'?"

"…No," Darkness answered, going for another dish. Beside her, Megumin was happily sipping at the blowfish stew.

Blowfish, huh…?

Come to think of it, I had never even had blowfish in Japan. "Darkness is right—everything else aside, you're pretty good at healing. Okay!"

"Uh, Kazuma, did you say 'everything else aside'?"

"…No. Wow! That's incredible!"

No sooner had I tried the stew than I was marveling at the flavor. I don't have a big vocabulary, so the best I could do was to describe it as absolutely delicious.

Aqua watched us with satisfaction. "I'm so pleased you're all enjoying it so much. That blowfish is from Cecily. She usually uses it to help convert new worshippers. You draw in passersby with blowfish, then you promise them antidote magic if they convert. It's a great strategy! But then Cecily got arrested…"

"That's what you've been up to? I thought I told you to stay away from that woman."

But either way, thanks to her, we got to eat Paradise Blowfish for dinner, and I admit I was grateful for that. I took one of the thin slices of sashimi, while Aqua cooked up one of the fins on the brazier and dropped it in her drink to make fin sake. Sitting there drinking with a side of blowfish roe, Aqua looked less like a goddess or even a heroine and more like a middle-aged guy at a bar.

"Come to think of it, aren't the internal organs supposed to be the most poisonous of all? Don't get carried away and eat too much. If *you're* paralyzed when we start to go numb, we're all done for."

"Don't be dumb; I'm wearing a divine item, you see? It neutralizes harmful status effects. Blowfish poison can't even touch me."

Come to think of it, I guess she had mentioned that once. Knowing her, I was afraid there was some flaw in her logic, but if she was right, then…!

I lost track of how much blowfish I'd enjoyed.

"Hef-hef-hef! How abouf thabh, Kafuma? Wiff my defenfe, I can enthure any poithon…"

"Her tongue is going numb. You can hear it," I said. Darkness had gorged herself on the most dangerous parts of the fish, and I was thinking it was about time to lay some healing magic on her.

Suddenly I felt something slumped against me. I looked over to find Megumin, her face flushed, leaning on my shoulder right there in front of everybody…

"Aqua, pay attention! Megumin'th almoth gone… Craf, I can harthly fpeak…"

I looked at Aqua, and my blood ran cold.

She was lying facedown on the table. What had happened to her divine item?! Didn't it work against poison?!

Darkness, picking up on the situation, rushed over and grabbed Aqua…!

"*Zzzzz.*"

"She's a lightweight drinker! Wake up! Waaaaghh uuupppp!"

4

The next morning.

"Hey, Kazuma, are you really going to take Lady Iris up on that quest? Let me tell you something: I think that even without your offensive attitude, it would be all we could do to survive an escort quest. I mean, our entire party was almost wiped out by the blowfish we had for our own dinner!"

"Yesterday doesn't count; we weren't on an adventure. We're the number one party in Axel. We've beaten more generals of the Demon King than anyone else in the world. I won't let anyone speak ill of us."

Yes, we had been brought to the brink of destruction by food poisoning the night before, but now we had made all our preparations to go to the capital and had come to Axel's transport shop.

We had rushed over to the Eris Church and somehow managed to survive, but I didn't plan on having any more blowfish for a while.

"Aqua's late. I thought she was only dropping off Chomusuke and Emperor Zel. I wonder if something happened to her."

The only thing we needed before we could leave was Aqua, who had gone to Wiz's place to drop off our pets. She was probably busy getting in a fight with Vanir or something.

As the thought crossed my mind, Aqua came up, loaded with luggage. "I dropped off the kids. Old Nasty Mask took one look at Chomusuke and started spouting off about *'Oh-ho, I look away for but an instant and another interesting thing befalls us! Bwa-ha-ha-ha-ha-ha-ha!'* Whatever, I guess it doesn't matter."

"Interesting thing"? I wondered what that could be. Maybe Chomusuke really would turn into that lady when she got bigger. I was dying to know more, but we had other things to do.

"Okay, guys, when we enter the transport shop, let me do the talking. I've been wanting to give them a piece of my mind for a long time now."

"A piece of your mind? Is there bad blood between you and the owner here?" Darkness asked, but instead of answering, I shoved open the door of the shop.

The seeds of my rage had been planted months before. This was after I had been forcibly separated from my little sister, Iris, and had tried to go visit her in secret.

"Hey, buddy, I'm back! Send us to the capital!"

"Come right i— Hey! You're that Kazuma Satou the police are after! You've got some nerve coming back here… I told you you're not allowed to travel to the capital!"

Darkness sounded downright frustrated at that. "Y-you dirty rotten— You tried to go visit Iris when I wasn't looking, didn't you?"

"Damn right I did. But they wouldn't let me. I'm sure Claire is behind it. But this time is gonna be different. Here, Buster, feast your eyes on this! A letter of invitation from the royal family! That's the real goods, so keep your grimy hands off!"

I proudly displayed the letter, but the owner of the transport shop just frowned. "Oh, is it, now? You didn't forge yourself a letter? Is this like the time you tried to intimidate me by telling me what awful things would happen to me if I tried to go against a close personal friend of House Dustiness?"

"Kazuma, come over here for a moment. I want to talk to you."

"No thanks. Listen, pal, funny you should mention the Dustinesses, because this is their daughter right here. Everyone in town knows her, right? So was I telling the truth or wasn't I?" I pulled back against Darkness, who was tugging on my arm. The owner's face went pale.

When Darkness saw that, she dragged me to a corner of the store with a burst of strength.

"I'll 'no thanks' you! Kazuma, have you been dropping my name to support your illicit activities? You haven't actually done anything illegal on the authority of my family name, have you?"

"Aqua and I went to a fancy restaurant, and when they tried to tell us we didn't meet the dress code, we mentioned your name. That's about it."

"When none of the carpenters in the area wanted to help renovate the Axis Church building, I said I would tell on them to you. That's about it."

"As for me, when I was buying something to go with dinner, I told them it was for the plate of Young Lady Lalatina and to please be sure to give me the most delicious part. That's about it."

Darkness went limper and limper with each of our reports. She had both her hands over her face. I wasn't sure if it was to keep herself from crying or to hide her embarrassment.

The shopkeeper gave Darkness a pitying look, then said gently, "I can tell from your reaction that you really are a member of the Dustiness family. Ahem, if this is indeed on the order of the royal family, then consider my services complimentary..."

"Cool, thanks."

"We'll pay! I'll pay you—I don't want to cause any more trouble for commoners!"

I was going to take him up on his generous offer, but Darkness bounded forward with her purse in her hand. "Just remember this, Kazuma. When this quest is over, I'm going to have a few questions to ask you. You too, Aqua and Megumin. Don't pretend like you're innocent here!"

The three of us joined the grumbling Darkness, squeezing into a magic circle.

"Bah, stubborn noble. We're party members. That practically makes us family, right? What's mine is yours and, more importantly, what's yours is mine. Remember that I'm the one who treats you perfectly normally even though you're a noble. That's how friends work. Whenever you need a hand, feel free to mention the name of the number one Adventurer in Axel."

"That's right, Darkness, and just tell me any time you need the power of the Axis Church. I'll be happy to help you."

"I was a little intimidated when I first learned you were a noble, Darkness, but now I see you simply as Darkness. Any time you need the help of the Crimson Magic Clan, you need merely ask. I can dispatch a letter back home immediately."

For a second, Darkness looked simultaneously embarrassed and happy. "Y-you guys…! …Huh? Wait, hold on, something's not right here! I mean, I don't see myself ever needing to drop Kazuma's name or lean on the power of the Axis Church or the strength of the Crimson Magic Clan…!"

The rest of us didn't really understand what she was talking about, but we got ready for our teleport.

Then it happened.

"Hey, hey, Kazuma, did you know? Every once in a greeeaaaat while, an accident happens during teleportation! Like, you get spliced together with something that happened to wander into the magic circle! They say that's how werewolves and lamia came to be! That's what I heard!"

I didn't know if she was trying to scare me or what, but…

"Fine, next time let's get a few goblins and throw them in there with you. If we're lucky, the splice might make you a little smarter."

"What's that, you stupid NEET? Well, we should teleport *you* with a hardworking ant; maybe it would curb your NEET-ness a little!"

"A-ahem… Teleportation accidents really are a genuine possibility, so please stop wrestling in the magic circle…"

The shopkeeper looked distressed; I just gave the *go* signal. "All right. Send us to the capital, old man!"

All the major quests I'd accepted up to this point, I had either been dragged into or stumbled on. But not this time. This time, I was going out of my refusal to hand my precious little sister over to some prince I'd never even met.

"H-hold on—!"

Darkness seemed to want to say her piece, but the shopkeeper was already chanting the spell.

"*Teleport!*"

1

Arriving in the capital by Teleport, we found ourselves in front of the royal castle for the first time in a while. Two guards stood by the entrance gate, giving us fishy looks.

"Halt! Authorized personnel only past this point! Adventurers should keep their distance!"

I showed the high-and-mighty guard my letter, complete with the royal seal. "I'm Kazuma Satou, an adventurer from Axel Town here on business for Princess Iris."

The sight of the royal seal sure changed their tune; the guards quickly straightened up. "P-pardon us, sir...! We'll summon our superior immediately; please wait here! May we bring your envelope with us?"

"I suppose so," I said, putting on some airs of my own. All it got me was a jab in the ribs from Darkness.

Inspecting the contents of the envelope, the guards happened to look at the letter. "Hey, this letter's been torn... What's going on...?"

"Uh, you can just ignore that! I mean, things happen when you're an adventurer, right? Monsters and stuff. I'm sure you understand!"

"Indeed, indeed... Let us show you to the waiting area."

I could hardly tell them that, enraged, I had shredded a letter from the royal family, but they seemed to buy my excuse, and one of the guards led us to a reception area.

We each took a seat, and I proceeded to squeeze the local gossip out of the guard, which he handed over eagerly. "Kazuma Satou is a name we've been hearing even here in the capital recently. After all, he helped Lady Dustiness lead a major battle on the front lines, bringing our forces to victory. You hear stories about the quick-witted, many-talented Kazuma, leader of a party that also includes the noble Crusader Lady Dustiness and an Arch-wizard who boasts incredible magic power, plus the plaster-monger they brought along."

"Say, do any of these rumors happen to mention a gorgeous Arch-priest?"

When you got right down to it, our party had defeated more generals of the Demon King than anyone else. It was actually weird that we weren't *more* famous.

"At the moment, the only two names that are widely known from the party are Mr. Kazuma and Lady Dustiness, but could it be that young woman over there is the great wizard, the user of Explosion? I can't imagine why someone who put on such an astonishing display should not have given her name. The rumors say you're a humble, mysterious personage who modestly shuns the spotlight…"

At the soldier's description, Megumin let the slightest smile creep onto her face. Maybe she thought she looked like someone really clever. She answered quietly, "…Ah, is that what the rumors say? Yes, I suppose I could be called humble. After all, I'm the one who has given Kazuma all the money I made on our adventures."

"Hey, no one's said *my* name yet. I'm famous all over this world, and I haven't heard my name yet."

I thought there was a very different reason Megumin didn't want her name to be widely known, but she was so taken with the idea of being mysterious and self-effacing that she had completely forgotten about it.

The soldier grew only more impressed. "I-incredible! So you're saying you have no interest at all in money or fame?!"

"Heh… The sole thing I seek is true mastery of magic. When

Kazuma begged me to join his party, this was what I said: *'I ask but a minimum of remuneration for sustenance and living. The only other thing I request is a chance to make the best use of my powers'...!"*

"Woooooow!"

The way I remember it was, when I threatened to kick her out of the party, she cried and begged me to let her stay, even if I paid her only a minimum for food and survival.

But at that moment…

"Ahhh! It really *is* you!"

Someone appeared in the doorway of the waiting area with an audible groan. I recognized the wizard who stood there with a hood hiding her face. It was Lain, the noblewoman who was also Iris's tutor and bodyguard.

"Of course it's me. Iris asked for me personally; did you know that? I've got to say, normally I would expect more, you know, awards and banquets for a party that's defeated yet another general of the Demon King."

"Urgh… W-well…" Lain blanched and looked away. Maybe it was a prick of conscience. It didn't last long, though: She grabbed Darkness's arm, pulled her out of the room, and had a hushed conversation in which they both kept stealing glances at me.

"Lady Dustiness, didn't you tell me you were going to find some way to refuse this request? Leaving Lady Iris in *his* hands is sure to create a diplomatic incident…!"

"Believe me, I tried, but his resistance was stronger than I expected. Luckily, he thinks he broke me, so his guard is down. When we get to the neighboring capital, I'll slip him something so he'll be asleep the entire time Lady Iris is there."

"Ooh, just the kind of brilliant plan I'd expect from you, Lady Dustiness! I can rest easy, then!"

…Those two were definitely plotting something. Did this mean that when Darkness had tied me up, it had been on orders from the state? And if you're wondering how I could even understand what they were whispering to each other…

"What's wrong, Kazuma? Why are you staring at those two so hard?"

"Oh, I was just checking out whether my newest skill works."

That's right: It was thanks to my new Read Lips skill. It allowed you to get the gist of someone's conversation from watching their mouths. I didn't have any big plans for it; I'd learned it mostly so I could kill time eavesdropping on the other adventurers at the Guild—but it was coming in handy.

Suddenly, there was a commotion outside the waiting room.

"Kazuma Satou! Is it true Kazuma Satou is here?!"

I knew that voice. It belonged to a woman I didn't always get along with.

We all looked over to see an imperious noble in her trademark white suit: Claire, Iris's bodyguard, came storming into the room.

The moment she saw me, Claire grabbed my arm and dragged me to a corner of the room.

"What's up, White Suit? Let me guess: You didn't want me here, either?"

I was on my guard, but Claire leaned in and whispered, "Don't call me 'White Suit,' you rogue. I'm actually glad you're here. I thank you for coming."

……

That only made me even more suspicious. "You're thanking me? What's going on? What are you planning?"

"I'm not planning anything… Okay, that's not entirely true. Here, I have something for you."

Claire took the sigil of her house that hung on a pendant around her neck and gave it to me. Darkness had one of those, too. It proved you were of noble birth, and it was extremely valuable.

"...Seriously, what's going on? What, have you secretly been in love with me this whole time? I hate to break it to you, but I've been getting in good with another girl. An upright and faithful man like me can't allow myself to go any further than this. I'm sorry, but you'll just have to give up on me."

"What idiotic fantasies are you having? And how can you shoot me down before I've even said anything?" Claire flinched when she realized how loud her voice had gotten. She glanced around and regained her composure. "The point is, I think we can cooperate this time. I know there are good political reasons for entertaining this match, but...personally, I'm fundamentally against the idea of Lady Iris's engagement."

"Go on."

Now she had my attention. Claire pulled something out of a pouch. "Lady Iris's intended is the first prince of our neighboring nation. His soft upbringing, however, has made him a spoiled brat. Lady Iris far exceeds him in her talent for battle, and he would never look right beside the sweetest and most beautiful princess in the entire world. Not to mention, Elroad belittles our nation. If Lady Iris was to marry into its aristocracy, I'm sure people would sneer at her as a country bumpkin behind her back... Hence why I'm giving you this."

Looking at me with something less than enthusiasm, Claire passed me a black pouch.

"What's this?"

"It's a powerful elixir nobles use when they wish to bury a political opponent..."

I sent the pouch flying as soon as it landed in my palm.

"Hey! Do you know how expensive that was?!"

"You can't make me your pet assassin! I'm more than happy to ruin this wedding, but I refuse to sacrifice myself in the process! I know what you really want. You want a good, clean way to kill me *and* Prince Jerkwad!"

Claire gave a little click of her tongue. "Fine. Then there's something I want to ask of you in addition to your bodyguard duties. So long as you have that necklace I gave you, you can exercise the authority of the Sinfonia house with impunity. In this one instance, consider my family to be your backers. I will *not* give Lady Iris to this nobody. Break this engagement any way you can."

"In that case, gladly. They won't make Iris unhappy on my watch. Just leave it to me. If this kid is as much of a little snot as you say, I'll do whatever it takes to stop this."

Claire's face lit up at my prompt reply. "I guess I misjudged you. Allow me to apologize for all my past rudeness. I'm entrusting the matter of Lady Iris to you."

"Nah, look, I'm sorry, too. I guess you really do care about Iris. I may not look like much, but I've faced down a lot of enemies way more dangerous than some punk prince. This one's in the bag."

Iris had been the cause of so much fighting between us, but in that instant, we buried the hatchet. Claire and I locked our hands in a firm shake.

"To me at this moment, you seem the most stalwart companion in this room. I can't leave this country, but there'll be a reward waiting for you when you get back."

"And me, I'm glad to have such a powerful supporter. As for my reward, when this is all over, let's grab a drink and you can tell me some hilarious stories about when Iris was a little girl."

"Ah, sir, there isn't an ounce of greed in you. I'll regale you with stories all night long. Little Lady Iris concealed a considerable talent for destruction."

Then, ignoring everyone else in the room, we shared a smile...

"You two sure seem to be getting along." The voice, almost sad, came out of the blue. I turned and saw a young girl just peeking through the doorway, fidgeting shyly.

The second Princess Iris met my eyes, she said bashfully, "It's been so long, Elder Brother. I've been so eager to see you...!"

2

We were led behind the royal castle, where we found ourselves standing in front of a carriage that looked plain and simple but was made of
sturdy stuff.

Well actually, *carriage* wasn't quite the right word. There were no
wheels and no horses to pull it.

"Lizard Runners! Kazuma, look, Lizard Runners!" Megumin
tugged excitedly on my sleeve.

Yes, attached to this carriage-ish thing were two lizards. Two of
the frilled freaks I'd once dealt with on a hunting quest, standing and
honking only a few feet away.

"Kyun kyun skreee!"

Megumin and Aqua were grinning at the creatures' shrieks, which
were admittedly pretty cute for such scary-looking monsters.

When Darkness saw the vehicle, she said, "Ugh, we're using one of
the royal lizard-drawn carriages? I thought this meeting was supposed
to be secret."

"A typical horse-drawn conveyance would take too long. The journey is ten days by conventional carriage, but this vehicle will get you
there in a fraction of the time." As she offered this explanation, Claire
mumbled something under her breath, then put a hand on the lizard
carriage. It rose several feet off the ground, then just floated there.

Ah, so that was why it didn't have any wheels. This way, there
would be hardly any resistance as the Lizard Runners pulled the carriage. It really would be faster.

"I don't know if I could survive ten days without seeing Lady Iris.
Let alone the twenty days a simple round trip would entail. So we're
doing this instead."

"Why don't you come with us already?" I said, not entirely face-
tiously, but Claire grimaced.

"You heard her. This trip is supposed to be kept quiet. If there was
too much of an entourage, people would start to wonder which noble

was making their way about. It's the same reason we've made the carriage so plain. What's more, the country needs me here to lead it. I have much work to do. My post can't be left vacant for so long."

Personally, I was a little worried for the nation's future with this lady in charge.

Just then, Darkness hopped up on the driver's bench and picked up the lizards' reins. Apparently, she was actually planning to be our driver. As a noble, she must know how to handle horses.

The only problem was, these weren't horses. But I didn't think she would like hearing that. So as concerned as I was about leaving our ride in her hands…

To my surprise, it looked like we were Iris's only bodyguards for this trip. I was sort of grateful: That meant fewer people to scold me if they thought I was being too friendly with Iris.

All the preparations had been made before we got there. Iris was in the carriage, dressed in armor worthy of a member of the royal family and carrying a sparkling sword. She was eager to get going. "Elder Brother, come over here! The seat next to me is open. We can play games on the way there, like the ones you taught me last time!"

"Oh? Eager to spend time with your big bro, huh, Iris? Well, Big Bro's eager to spend time with you, too!"

Iris patted the seat beside her excitedly. She must have been really lonely, not seeing me for so long. She seemed way friendlier than when we had said good-bye last time.

Megumin, who had climbed in behind me, shoved her face up close to Iris's. "Hey, it is unheard of for a minion to claim the best seat! This spot behind the driver's bench with its excellent view, I call for myself! Give it to me, or I won't invite you to play anymore!"

"Th-that's no fair! That has nothing to do with this, and today, I'm not a minion, I'm a princess! I'm big and important! I won't give you this spot, and if you want it, you can fight me for it!"

I could've sworn they hadn't seen each other in a long time. And I had no idea what they were talking about. Claire and Lain just put their heads in their hands as if this was par for the course.

"...Hey, Darkness, you guys haven't been visiting Iris without telling me, have you? It seems like these two got awfully close outta nowhere."

"N-no, nothing of the sort... What really bothers me is Megumin referring to Lady Iris as a 'minion.'"

We stared at the girls questioningly, but in any event, they seemed to have settled their seating dispute.

"Very well, then, Iris and I shall share the spots behind the driver's bench."

"Yes, and you won't beat me on the way there. Whoever loses this game has to listen to the person who wins!"

Huh?

"Uh, I thought you were fighting over who got to sit next to me. So how did this happen?"

Incidentally, the lizard-drawn carriage could seat four. The interior boasted two benches for two people each.

"I'll sit next to Darkness. After all, what I want most is to see the scenery go by." Aqua, eager for the view, clambered up beside our driver. That left me by myself.

Huh? This can't be right.

What happened to my elegant, sexy trip?

As I grumbled and climbed into the carriage, Claire came up to Iris. "Lady Iris, have you forgotten anything? Do you have your handkerchief? Some pocket change in case there's an emergency? Don't hesitate to use any of the scrolls or magic items I gave you if you need them, okay? And if you get lonely, please, please try not to cry..."

"Claire, I'm not a little girl anymore. I'll be fine. In fact, if you don't let go of me, we won't be able to get started..."

Claire was giving Iris a hug from which she didn't seem to have any intention of releasing her; Lain finally pried her away from the princess. "Very well, Lady Iris. Try not to overexert yourself, and have a safe trip!"

"Kazuma Satou, I'm trusting you with Lady Iris! You have my permission to slice up any impertinent goon who tries to lay a finger on her! ...Lady Iriiiiiiiis!"

Iris looked at the two women bidding her farewell. "I'll see you both later!" she said with a wave.

Darkness gave a snap of the reins, and the Lizard Runners started running!

3

This quest was going to be half work, half travel—a nice, easy carriage ride.

Or so I thought...

"Waaaaaaaah, Kazuma! Kazumaaaaa!! Change seats with me! This is terrifying!"

"Whoa, aren't we going a little fast? If we get in an accident, we're all gonna die!"

Aqua was worse than surprised by the Lizard Runners' speed, and I added my own shouts to the commotion. With the carriage floating on thin air, the Runners reached an almost frightening speed.

"It's all right, Kazuma—royal lizard-drawn carriages are reinforced with powerful barriers. Even if we do get in an accident, only the driver's bench will be crushed. Ha-ha-ha-ha, this is fantastic! These are the best Lizard Runners I've ever seen! Onward, you beasts! Faster, faster!"

"Stop! Please let me back in the carriage!"

Darkness seemed unusually excited, and Aqua was about to break into tears; meanwhile, Iris and Megumin were playing like children.

"Kazuma, Kazuma! Look, some manticores are doing it over there!"

"Wh-where?! I wanna see manticores!"

The girls were all but climbing over each other to look out the window. Maybe they had forgotten their game in the face of the scenery whipping by, or maybe this was the first trip like this they had taken.

"You don't want to see manticores; you want to see animals doing it," said Megumin. "Sheesh. We have one noblewoman trying to put the moves on Kazuma and now a perverted little royal… I really wonder if this country is going to survive."

"The royal family isn't perverted! Or…little. Who was this noble-woman who tried to put the moves on Elder Brother? Could it be…?"

Darkness, finding herself under the scrutiny of the two excitable children, blushed.

"Hey, uh, what happens if a monster hits us while we're going this speed?! I'll have you know that if a revered entity like me goes splat, this world is going to end! Darkness, are you listening to me?!"

"Stop fretting, Aqua. This carriage is equipped with monster-repelling magical items, so it would very rarely encounter a monster. Just so long as our luck isn't exceptionally bad…"

"Kazuma, did you hear Darkness trip that flag?! Pleeeease let me into the carriage!"

I never expected a royal bodyguard mission to be so noisy. Was it going to be like this every day? For that matter, I was just noticing that we hadn't done any actual bodyguarding.

I was really starting to worry, but then my concerns were literally blown away.

"*Exterion!*"

Iris shouted, and the sword she was holding produced a glowing slash.

It was exactly the sort of awesome finishing move a great hero in a manga or a game would have, and it sliced the bull-like monster in front of us clean in two.

Maybe Darkness really had tripped a flag, because we had found our path blocked by a herd of monsters. We obviously couldn't simply plow right through them, so we stopped the carriage, assuming that all we had to do was jump out and exterminate them…

I beckoned Darkness over. "What's going on? Why is Iris so strong? If she's got moves like that, why are we even here?"

"Lady Iris is part of the royal family. The imperial line and some of the more prominent noble houses have gone out of their way over the ages to bring powerful heroes into their bloodlines, drastically increasing their powers. Plus, they get the best education in every field. *And* they have a near-limitless supply of the most XP-rich food, so they can raise their level constantly, and they fight with powerful weapons bequeathed to them by those heroes. Didn't you know that His Majesty and the first prince are fighting on the front lines even now?"

I obviously didn't. Anyway, if they were so strong, why didn't the royal family just go take out the Demon King?

I'd *thought* it was strange that we were the only bodyguards. As I recoiled slightly at the show of strength, Iris came up to me, grinning from ear to ear and clasping her sword to her chest. "What did you think of that, Elder Brother? I really tried my hardest!"

When she looked at me, desperate for validation, pretty much everything else faded into insignificance. "That's my little sister," I said. "Maybe you're not quite at my level (I've dealt with a lot of generals of the Demon King, after all), but strength like that definitely earns a passing grade. Let's keep up the good work."

"I don't know where you get your confidence, Elder Brother, but let me handle things! I can use this sacred treasure, passed down through my family generation after generation, to sweep away any monsters that try to get their hands on us! Just watch me!"

Did this kid say "sacred treasure"...?

"Hey, tell me about that sword. It looks super expensive, and it's, like…glowy."

"What, this? It's a national treasure: Something-calibur. I guess it's a divine treasure that protects the user from all kinds of status ailments and curses? I thought the scabbard was really pretty, so I bugged Daddy until he let me have it."

The name "Something-calibur" rang a bell with me. It reminded me of something Megumin had scribbled on me when I died once.

For that matter, that sword was famous. Was there anyone in the world who didn't know about it?

Megumin, whom I normally would have expected to be complaining about having her moment stolen by the grinning Iris, seemed in surprisingly high spirits.

"I expect no less from my minion and left hand. Anywhere we may find monsters, please continue to slice them apart just so."

"Yes! Leave it to me!"

You've got that backward. "Leave it to me"? We're supposed to be the bodyguards here!

"Hey, Megumin, what's all this 'minion' and 'left hand' business? Have you been up to some shenanigans while my back was turned? I've got a bad feeling asking this, but you've only been exchanging letters with Iris, right?"

"Shenanigans? I resent that. Everything we are doing is upright and just. All I have done recently is work with my right hand and left hand to set up a base and extend our territory. Maybe when our organization grows large enough, we'll even let you in, Kazuma."

So she was playing around building some secret hideout or something with her friends. She still had this really childish side to her, even if she did know how to make my heart beat out of my chest when we were alone...

4

Day one of our trip to the neighboring country.

To be honest, I never expected Iris to be so strong.

It was getting dark, so we decided to set up camp for the night. We had just climbed out of the lizard-drawn carriage.

"You're really something, Lady Iris. You must have worked so hard to get that strong." Darkness sounded like an older sister complimenting her younger sibling: Iris had buried all the monsters we'd met on the way almost as soon as we saw them.

Yep. Her so-called bodyguards were nothing more than an audience. Not that I objected to a nice, easy ride on Iris's coattails.

No, I didn't object, but as her older brother, I hated to, y'know, see my awesomeness take such a hit…

"I seem to recall you helped me train once, Lalatina. I hope you can see how strong it made me. I give you my thanks, Lalatina."

"Heh-heh! Think nothing of it, Princess."

Iris sounded almost shy; Darkness smiled to receive her ruler's praise.

……

"Didn't you tell me once that House Dustiness was charged with protecting the royal family? But you didn't protect anyone today. You *got* protected the whole time."

"?!" Darkness froze at my casual invective. "I d-don't know what you're talking about. I thought nice, easy monsters like the ones we saw today would be excellent combat practice for Lady Iris…!"

She couldn't hide the tremor in her voice, but Iris was quick to interject. "Elder Brother, Lalatina is the royal family's protector in emergencies. She is our nation's armor and shield. There was no need to bother Lalatina with such trivial opponents. If I was ever truly in need, I'm sure she would jump to my aid!"

"L-Lady Iris…!" Darkness clung to the little girl, deeply moved; Iris patted her head to comfort her. A moment ago, Darkness had looked like Iris's proud older sister, but now it was impossible to say who was older and who was younger.

One thing was for sure: Darkness was just as much of a handful as ever. The rest of us ignored her and started setting up camp.

When I thought about it, I realized this was the first serious camping we had ever done. We didn't normally get too far from home. I had missed my chance to strut my stuff as a bodyguard, so I would really have to kill the whole setting-up-a-tent thing to get my clout as Big Bro back.

While I was getting fired up for camping, Darkness, who seemed to have gotten herself back under control, pulled out some sort of magical item–looking thing.

"I'll prepare our lodgings, Lady Iris, so please step back."

With that, she tossed a square object into the closest clearing. It sparkled and instantaneously expanded into a small but obviously noble mansion.

"...Okay, what?"

"What do you mean, 'what'? Surely you don't imagine the princess of a major country would sleep in the dirt? This is one of the most valuable magical items the country possesses, thoroughly fortified against monsters, highly portable..."

"Just forget about all that already! Seriously, why the hell are we even here?!"

I might have been angry enough to interrupt Darkness's explanation of her little toy, but there was no question that the mansion was nicer than sleeping in a tent. It even had a garage attached for the carriage. We went inside, stashed our bags, and then got down to the business of relaxing.

My one little act of defiance was to insist that I do the cooking using my skill. The rest of the crew was searching through the house, deciding which rooms they wanted.

I figured, Iris being a princess, she might be getting tired of sumptuous banquets every day. I would make her something she wouldn't normally get to eat.

I took stock of the kitchen, including the available ingredients. There was no way sewers or running water existed in the middle of the wilderness like this, yet when I turned on the faucet, water came happily burbling out. Frankly, it was enough to kind of tick me off.

A voice came from behind me. "Elder Brother, could I help you in any way?"

I turned around to see Iris poking her head around the door of the kitchen.

"Can't ask a princess to help in the kitchen, can I? You just sit back and watch what I can do."

"A princess can at least help a little! They *never* let me help cook at the castle, no matter how many times I ask. Leave it to the servants, they say..."

She looked so downcast. I felt a little guilty.

Of course they wouldn't let a sheltered child like her do any cooking.

...*Okay.*

"All righty, then, maybe you can help a little. But cooking isn't as easy as it looks, okay? Be sure to do what I say and be careful not to get hurt."

"Sure thing, Elder Brother!"

I almost went weak in the knees when I saw how her face lit up. I looked through the magical refrigerator to find some ingredients she could prep easily. I needed a recipe she wouldn't be familiar with but that was simple enough for me to handle.

"Okay then, we're gonna do fried rice and pot stickers."

"Right! Um...*fryed rise* and *pot sticklers*? What kind of food is that?"

I grabbed a cabbage out of the refrigerator. "Fried rice is fried rice. They say there isn't a person alive who doesn't love fried rice, even if sheltered girls like you and Darkness might not know about it."

"Is it really that popular? I'm sorry to say I really don't know about it. Please enlighten me!"

Basking in Iris's reverent gaze, I felt myself starting to grin a little as I slapped the cabbage down on a cutting board. "First, we make the filling for the pot stickers! That means cabbage, chives, ground meat... Eeeyikes!"

"Oh no, the cabbage!"

The cabbage on the cutting board had only been playing dead. The moment I tried to bring my knife down on it, it flew away and darted out the open window. I'd left the window open to vent any smoke, but it had come back to bite me.

"...So you see, Iris, keeping your guard up while cooking is a matter of life and death. Just keep that in mind."

"Elder Brother, I may not know much, but even I know you have to make sure to check whether the food's still alive!"

That night.

"Kazuma, what have you served us? I've never seen this before." Darkness was intrigued by the stuff on the table.

After the incident with the first head of cabbage, and an epic struggle with a second, and Iris being viciously ambushed by the onions we were going to put into the fried rice, and a few other little hiccups besides, we successfully prepared fried rice and pot stickers, along with some egg soup.

"Lalatina, this is called fried rice. It is said there isn't a person alive who doesn't love it," Iris informed her. "I helped prepare it myself!"

"You did?! Well, what a hard worker. I can't wait to try it."

Darkness smiled broadly to see Iris so proud of her work. I tried a quick bite, too, and was pleased with what we had made. Iris and Darkness, though, were reflecting on the food with genuine seriousness.

"Lalatina, I can see why this dish is so popular. All one does to make this 'fried rice' is cook it over a fire, yet the flavor is so complex."

"There are no expensive ingredients in this, are there? I can't imagine why something so delicious never became popular among the noble families..."

Uh, probably because if you served pot stickers and fried rice at some fancy imperial banquet, someone would flip a table over?

The two guileless girls savored this most common of meals and turned admiring eyes on me. Meanwhile, I could feel Aqua and Megumin watching me with distinctly less respectful looks.

"Say, Kazuma, let me cook tomorrow night. I'll make something super-delicious for you."

"Well then, the day *after* tomorrow shall be my turn to cook. I shall serve a dish widely beloved in Crimson Magic Village."

With Megumin, it was one thing, but Aqua normally hated to cook. Huh. Well, there was plenty of trip left. I was grateful for the help.

"Hey, Kazuma, this 'potato chip' dessert of yours is divine."

"Yes, I can't stop eating them!"

As I watched the two girls enjoy the post-meal junk food, my thoughts turned to the journey ahead.

5

"Come on, Elder Brother—hurry up! Let's do more cooking!"

It was the next evening. Iris had once again kicked the butts of every monster that got in our way. The only thing of any note that happened was when her performance spurred Megumin to compete by letting off an explosion.

"You sure are getting into this, Iris," Aqua said. "I like your spunk. I'm going to show you something extra special tonight!"

"Really? Thank you so much! I promise to work hard!"

Iris and I weren't the only ones in the kitchen. Aqua had joined us. And frankly, I was a little annoyed. Megumin I could ignore, but Aqua seemed intent on teaching our unworldly companions, Iris and Darkness, the strangest things while we were on this trip.

Speaking of Megumin, who had used up all her magic, Darkness was keeping her company.

Aqua peered into the refrigerator and pulled out an assortment of ingredients.

"Tonight's dinner is tuna-mayo rice!"

She grinned broadly, hands on her hips.

Was she insane?

It was bad enough I had given the princess fried rice. We were going to pay for this later.

"Another dish I've never heard of. Are all of Elder Brother's acquaintances so knowledgeable?"

"You don't get to be an Arch-priest as great as I am without learning a thing or two, see? This is a nice, quick dish you can make when you're in a hurry. That's very important for adventurers, for whom even a second of inattention can be the difference between life and death, understand?"

"I see! A meal for busy adventurers!"

Aqua was hardly done with her absurd explanation before she had shredded the tuna and slapped it on the rice with some mayonnaise.

"Finished!"

"Very simple!"

Not to sound like a broken record, but was she insane?

She seemed to realize that maybe fish, rice, and condiments weren't enough for a meal, because she was rooting around in the refrigerator...

"I don't think this'll cut it by itself. I'll make you some dry-seasoned rice and some egg-fried rice to go with it."

"Of course! I can't wait!" Iris was looking at the tuna-mayo rice with keen interest and smiling enthusiastically.

When I finished bringing everyone's food to the table, I found the two "young ladies" once again examining their dinner, deeply intrigued.

"Lalatina, did you know you can make this dish in the blink of an eye? It hardly takes a full minute to prepare."

"Is that true, Lady Iris? Hey, Kazuma, why didn't you ever tell us there was such convenient food around? This stuff would be worth it for ease of preparation alone."

I think everyone but you already knows about it.

"You can put soy sauce or salt or even hot sauce on your rice for a totally fresh experience," Aqua said, pouring hot sauce on her food and then eating it as gracefully as if it was some hoity-toity gourmet thing.

"...Aqua, I always took you for just a simple know-nothing,

honestly. But I see now that appearances can be deceiving. Forgive me for being so shallow." Darkness, who was eating her rice the same way—that is to say, like a noble—bowed her head.

"You have a lot left to learn about the world. You and Iris are both sheltered young ladies, so it's only natural. When the time comes, I'll teach you all sorts of useful things, like how to get all the ice cream off the lid of an ice-cream cup."

Just *knowing* that seemed like something that would make an aristocrat mad at you. I wanted to cut in with a smart remark, but Iris and Darkness were looking at Aqua with such admiration that I didn't want to spoil the moment.

I, meanwhile, was eating my tuna-mayo rice with appropriate enjoyment, but Megumin was wolfing it down like it was a feast. I was starting to worry about what we would be served the next evening, but more to the point, the day after tomorrow, we would arrive in the capital of Elroad.

It would be fine. Megumin would be cooking for only one night. And she wasn't a terrible chef.

Yeah, it would be just fine…

6

"It went that way, Iris! Try not to let it pinch your fingers!"

"Got it—leave it to me! Oh, there's another lobster between the rocks!"

One more day till we reached Elroad.

We had spotted a river as we traveled and took a short break there at Megumin's insistence.

"This lobster seems awfully small, Megumin. Are we really going to eat this? I think it's still a baby. Oh! Ow-ow-owww…" Darkness was up to her thighs in the water, and now she was up to her finger in lobster claw. The weird note of happiness in her voice was totally typical, though.

"That is not a baby lobster. We are not in the big, wide sea here but in a shallow river, so they won't get any bigger than that. Oops, you're not getting away! That makes four!" Megumin had flipped over a rock and grabbed what she found there.

Yep:

"Hey, Kazuma. There's something I'd like to say…"

"Well, don't. Those are lobsters they're catching. Just the kind of expensive feast fit for a princess. Okay?"

We were busy catching crawfish.

I should have been suspicious the moment Megumin said she wanted to make food from Crimson Magic Village. She'd lived her entire life in poverty. What would she know about fancy food?

"Perhaps it's the lack of human travel that has allowed these fish to grow so big! This will make for a fabulous dinner!"

"Gosh, I've never gathered my own ingredients before! Who knew cooking could be so much fun?!"

"M-Megumin, grab this thing for me! It's got a hold on my toe…!"

Our two sheltered girls really seemed to be enjoying themselves. Maybe they didn't get to play in the water very much.

Me, I simply watched the peaceful scene. "The royal attendants went to so much trouble to stock up our refrigerator. I'm gonna make sure their efforts don't go to waste."

"Oh, no, you're not getting away. One less person means the rest of us each have to eat more food."

Finally, the sun went down, and we started to settle in for the night.

"Very well, Iris, are you ready? Now you shall see how *I* prepare a meal!"

"Of course! I can't wait!"

Megumin, standing in front of a pile of crawfish, was almost vibrating with excitement. She was even more eager to cook than usual, desperate to show Iris what she could do. "Normally one would soak them in water all night to expunge the mud, but the river in which we caught these crawfish was exceedingly clean, and there was no mud. We can get started immediately."

"This is very educational!"

And so Megumin went about teaching the young princess how to cook crawfish. I would have to have a word with Iris later so she didn't go blabbing to anyone at the capital that this was the sort of thing she had learned on her trip.

"Now, first we must remove the smell from the craw—er, lobsters. You simply need to submerge them in alcohol, such as... Ah yes, this will do." Megumin pulled a bottle of wine out of the fridge and emptied it into a bowl—expensive wine that *someone* had been looking forward to drinking, but I pretended I hadn't seen it. "Now we leave them for a few minutes until the stink is replaced by a fragrant aroma. We can do some other preparations while we wait..."

Megumin directed things with all the grace you would expect of someone who had cared for her own little sister. Iris looked at her with genuine respect.

"Whoops, I seem to have done it all myself. Well, this should be enough preparation. Next..."

Megumin had been enjoying Iris's admiring look so much that she had accidentally done everything herself. She quickly snapped back to taking cooking seriously. She started with crawfish soup, then grilled a few more of them, and then made a spicy sauce to go over the rest.

When she was finished with this surprising display of domestic capability, Megumin exhaled in satisfaction. "Kazuma has been doing all the cooking lately. I wish you would all have some of my food from time to time. Here, Iris, at least help set the table."

"Oh, of course! I'm sorry—I just couldn't take my eyes off you..."

"Ah, well, I suppose I can forgive you for a fixation on your leader! Okay, I'll set the table, too—you go wash your hands."

I had never seen this side of Megumin before.

"Hey, what's this 'leader' stuff?" I demanded.

"…Nothing."

"This is fantastic. The richness of freshly caught lobster just fills the soup, making it savory and complex. And the slight touch of earthiness left in the meat perfectly complements the grilling; nothing to object to there. This is true mastery…!"

Darkness was savoring her food, acting like the narrator on some cooking show. She was trying to sound like a gourmand, but I wanted to point out to her that she wasn't eating lobster but the common crawfish.

Iris, still on a high from the unfamiliar experience of catching her own ingredients, looked thrilled, too.

Megumin, claiming that she had actually made too much, had gone to share some of the food with the Lizard Runners.

…In other words, if I wanted to do something about this, now was my chance.

"Say, Kazuma, for some reason I feel like having frogs today. I'm going to go cook up those frogs they left in the refrigerator, so here—you can have my crawfish."

"My dear departed grandpa died when he went out to check the fields one day and was attacked by a gang of crawfish. I haven't been able to eat shellfish since. So please, Aqua, have my share."

…………

"Do you think you can deceive the eyes of a goddess? I know your grandpa came rushing to the hospital when you almost got run over by that tractor! And anyway, you sure like our speckled crabs well enough!"

"And what about you? So you just feel like having frogs, huh? That's rich, coming from someone who almost got eaten by one!"

We were right in the middle of our attempts to shove food onto each other's plates when we felt a presence behind us.

It was Megumin, back from feeding the lizards.

"Hey now, if you have a complaint about my family's treasured secret recipe, I shall hear it."

"Aw, it was just a joke. We're happy to eat your food."

"Yeah, we were just horsing around. This shrimp looks great; maybe I'll try some of this."

Aqua and I steeled ourselves to have some food. Why not? This wasn't crawfish; it was lobster. And anyway, I'd been eating frogs since I got to this world. Why worry about some crawfish now? Plus, crawfish had originally been imported as food…

"Whoa, these aren't half-bad. Kazuma, give me yours. I brought some expensive wine to keep me company on this trip. I need something to eat with it, so leave me your crawfish."

……

As I watched Aqua head happily off to the kitchen to get her wine out of the refrigerator, I promptly popped a crawfish into my mouth.

"…Huh, that's pretty good. The shell is crisped exactly right. And it's melted into the soup perfectly. No wonder your family values this recipe so highly. I'm sorry I made fun of your craw—I mean, lobsters."

"Oh, I just wanted to try calling something a treasured family recipe for once in my life. If you're enjoying it, that's what counts."

…I immediately regretted my attempt to be nice by praising Megumin's cooking.

From the kitchen, I could hear Aqua sobbing.

7

That night.

Having to use an unfamiliar pillow always made it hard for me to sleep. The constant stress of our high-speed, lizard-based travel wore on my nerves enough that I was able to fall asleep pretty easily each night, but by the third day, it seemed I had gotten used to it.

I got out of bed and went to the kitchen in search of water.

*   *   *

"*Freeze.*"

Thanks to my ability to see in the dark, I didn't even need to turn on the kitchen lights as I went to the faucet and got a drink. I slugged it down and let out a breath…and that was when I felt something behind me.

There was only one person I could think of who could see in the dark like I could: the one who had been reduced to tears by having her special wine used up…

"Is that you, Elder Brother?"

But I was wrong.

In the darkness, illuminated only by the wisps of starlight that came in through the window, there was Iris standing in the kitchen doorway.

"Yeah, it's me; it's your elder brother. I wanted some water. I just can't seem to get to sleep."

Iris let out a relieved breath when she heard my voice. "Um, I came to powder my nose, but it's dark… Could you walk me back to my room?"

She kept her eyes fixed on what she could see of my face, reaching out hesitantly to take my hand. I mean, sure, she could've simply turned on a light, but this was the girl who had spent her entire young life suppressing anything resembling a selfish urge. She was probably afraid to turn on a light lest she wake anyone up.

"Sure, I'm on it. Elder Brother can take you to your room. If you're feeling scared of the dark, I can even hop in bed with you."

"I'll be fine, thanks."

………

I took Iris's small, slender hand and walked out into the dark corridor. Iris was walking as quietly as she could, maybe so she wouldn't wake anyone up. Creeping through the dark while everyone else slept, trying to make ourselves as inconspicuous as possible, it almost felt like we were doing something wrong.

Suddenly, Iris squeezed my hand. I looked over at her. She seemed to feel the same way I did, like we had stumbled into a little prank while sneaking out for a midnight snack. "This reminds me of that time I came to your room one night so you could tell me stories about your past, Elder Brother."

"Oh, you mean when you showed up without getting Claire's permission? She almost had my head the next day. She acted like I'd kidnapped you or something."

During my time in the capital, Iris had occasionally given Claire the slip and come to see me. It caused an uproar in the castle each time. Maybe that was the real number one reason I'd been barred from the city?

Iris, smiling, interrupted my thoughts. "But you never acted like it was any trouble when I showed up. You just talked to me... I still remember, you know. Your story about the time you fought with the cross-bearing demon—I mean Santa Claus, the one you say shows up in your country and leaves despair in the stockings of all the single people."

Ahhh, my little sister was so smart. She remembered even the things I'd said half as a joke.

"I haven't forgotten. And I remember how you told me about the time in your life you spent battling day and night, until people dubbed you the MMO Monster."

Ahhh, my little sister was so naive. She bought my NEET stories hook, line, and sinker and still looked at me with utmost respect.

...Actually, I was feeling pretty awful about that.

My silence seemed to send the wrong message to Iris, who said anxiously, "I'm sorry. Did I make you homesick, talking about all that?"

No, not at all. You just made me take a long, hard look at myself.

But I couldn't say that, so I simply smiled instead. "Nah, I was just feeling kind of sentimental. I really enjoyed those days."

I knew she couldn't see my expression in the dark, but she could still tell I was smiling. She seemed relieved.

"That's good to hear. Um..."

Before I knew it, we found ourselves standing at the door to her room. She let go of my hand and opened the door, then glanced my way for only a second.

"Please, Elder Brother, I hope you'll stay in my country forever. I'll work hard to make our nation somewhere you'll always want to be."

It was like she just knew somehow that something was going to take me far away. She smiled, but it seemed awfully sad.

8

Next morning.

Aqua was almost beside herself knowing we would get to Elroad today. I was weirdly bothered by what Iris had said the night before, though, so when I climbed up on the driver's bench beside Darkness, I asked her about it.

"Hey, Darkness, this trip is about seeing this little punk Iris is supposed to marry, right? We just say hi, and then we can go home, right?"

Darkness looked at me in annoyance, then glanced surreptitiously at Iris, who was playing with Aqua and Megumin. "You really think this is just a meet and greet? If that was true, why on earth would we do it so secretly, and right when the Demon King's attacks are ramping up? I'll tell you why we're going there: to beg Elroad for help."

Beg for help.

"Like, we want them to send us big, bad adventurers or knights or something?"

"No, every country around has already done that for us. We're the only country that shares a border with the Demon King's army, see? If we fall, the whole defensive line collapses, and the Demon King marches right into the soft underbelly of our neighboring nations. So they send us their best troops whenever they can."

Huh.

"But this country we're going to, Elroad —the knights there are pushovers the way only knights from a country built on gambling could be. Elroad provides us financial support instead of military support. They help substantially with defraying the costs of defense."

"Huh, okay. But what does that have to do with this trip?"

"Remember when I said the Demon King's attacks are getting worse? There's a reason for that. Kazuma…I believe we've defeated too many of his generals."

…

"What? He wants revenge for his minions?"

"It's not that. The Demon King's army is starting to panic. Their generals were all but invincible until recently, and now they're dropping like flies. So we've decided not only to firm up our defenses but also to try to make a positive attack. But believe it or not, Elroad is claiming a cash crunch and saying that not only can't they afford to support an offensive but they even want to stop paying for our defense. His Majesty and the first prince are away doing battle, so Lady Iris is going there to negotiate."

"…Wow, okay." I finally started to understand Iris's comment from the previous night. She was afraid that if the military situation got worse, I might flee somewhere safer.

So she was going to be married off to Elroad in exchange for monetary support. Considering that my little sister was the cutest thing in the whole wide world, at least she wouldn't have any trouble convincing them to take her.

"Our country has a long-standing friendship with Elroad. We complement each other perfectly: Belzerg is militarily strong but doesn't do much trade, while Elroad is vulnerable to attack but knows how to make a buck. I don't care how cash-strapped they are. The fate of our nation and our world is riding on this visit. So *please* don't cause any trouble." Darkness stared me straight in the eyes.

"…All right. For the sake of this world and all humankind. I'm an adventurer; I've fought the Demon King's forces. Even I know better than to put myself ahead of beating him. I know sometimes things can't change, no matter how much you beg and plead. So don't worry so much." I smiled as reassuringly as I could.

Darkness didn't look like she quite believed me.

"Hey, what's with that face? You don't think I mean it?"

"I'm just trying to believe I'm even hearing talk from you about helping the world and humankind… Well, whatever. When we get to Elroad's castle town, we can start by taking a little break. We can't show up at the castle the minute we get there anyway. We'll rest up and then get down to business."

Then she tried to smile comfortingly at me…

……*Ahhh, I get it.*

I remembered the conversation she'd had with Lain before we left, the one about drugging me so I would spend the whole time asleep.

There was a commotion behind us.

"Oh! Kazuma, Kazuma, look! There's Elroad—you can see it!"

"Ah-ha-ha-ha-ha-ha! Finally! Elroad, the land of my dreams, the country of casinos!"

Up in the front seat, Darkness and I traded highly questionable smiles with each other.

1

Other nations referred to this one as Elroad, the Casino Kingdom.

Arriving in the capital, we were flabbergasted by the crowds and the noise.

"Hey, Kazuma, Axel hardly gets this many people for a festival! Where have they all come from?"

We were traveling down a big, wide street, so our carriage was limited to the speed of the people around us. Aqua was eagerly observing those people from the driver's bench, looking this way and that and snickering at everyone going by.

"Aqua," I said, "this is supposed to be a secret trip, remember? So don't go drawing attention to yourself. Don't forget why we're here."

Aqua pretty much ignored my attempt to rein her in; she was more interested in the open-air establishments we were passing.

It wasn't like I couldn't sympathize. It was as crowded as Shibuya Scramble Crossing in Japan. And this world's population was a lot smaller than Earth's. So to have this many people in one place meant...

"This must be a disinformation plot, an attempt to make people think this capital is thriving. Look, you see that guy who just went around the corner? I guarantee he'll go around the block and come straight back. They're all plants. Everyone here has been hired to mill around."

"I knew you were a sharp one, Kazuma. I thought something was strange, too. After all, if this was all real, it would make our home base in Axel look like a cow town."

Darkness blushed slightly as she heard Aqua and me chatting with each other. "Both of you, stop your ridiculous jabbering and act grown-up. I couldn't stand anyone thinking we were country bumpkins."

Which was exactly how she was treating us, but what were you gonna do? The shops and stalls along the street were crammed with foods I had never seen before, the shopkeepers hawking their wares at the top of their lungs.

The lizard-drawn carriage pulled to a stop in front of a larger building along the same street. Someone must have made reservations for us in advance.

"All right, this is our inn," Darkness said. "Everyone, go drop off your traveling stuff. Lady Iris's meeting with the prince is scheduled for tomorrow. Today we can rest up and take in the sights."

Someone from the inn came out and took the carriage off our hands.

We were mostly on cloud nine, but Iris shook her head. "I have to get ready for the conference tomorrow… And I have to admit, I'm a little bit nervous, meeting this prince for the first time. I'm going to rest here and try to prepare myself. You all have fun." Then she grabbed her luggage.

"Lady Iris, were you not looking forward to this excursion? We're your bodyguards; we can't leave you alone at—"

"Y-you have to! Get some rest. We came all this way to the Casino Kingdom. I couldn't relax if I knew you were stuck at the inn with me!"

Knowing how sensitive Iris was to the feelings of those around her, I knew she probably really would be driven to distraction by us staying with her.

"Come on, Darkness—you heard the lady. Let's go stretch our wings."

"Ugh... O-okay, fine..." She still didn't sound completely convinced, but she nodded anyway, seeming a little overwhelmed by Iris, whose smile looked like it concealed a very powerful resolve.

We set down our bags in our rooms.

"Casino! Let's hit the casino! Then, after we win big, we can use the money to take a food tour! I'll bet you can get some *really* good wine around here!"

"No, let us go to the local equipment shop! I'm sure I will be able to find an exceptionally powerful staff suitable for myself!"

We went right back out into town.

"Hrm, I'm still not entirely comfortable leaving Lady Iris behind like this..."

Darkness was the only member of our party who wasn't completely on board.

Iris seemed really stressed about this meeting she was supposed to have. Maybe she was doing a sort of simulation by herself rather than going out and playing. I was concerned that trying to be too considerate would backfire. I would bring her a nice souvenir instead.

But even so...

"You guys need to think things through. We came all this way, so let's start with the famous tourist destinations. Even Crimson Magic Village had a few, so a place like this must—"

—*have some cool stuff.*

Is what I was about to say, but just then...

"Ooh? Lookit that lovely adventurer. Hey, you blond-haired beauty, how about you ditch the wimp and come hang out with some real men?"

"Yowza, what a bunch of hotties! I'm all about that blue-haired lady!"

"The chick with black hair and red eyes is doin' it for me..."

We passed by a few guys being extra sleazy. They each looked a year or two older than me. They were wearing the sort of gaudy outfits guys wear when they're clearly peacocking, and they were leering openly at us. They were all thin and gangly; they looked like rich cream puffs who had come to the city for a little fun.

As for my companions, whom the three guys had been catcalling...

""" ...?"""

Each of them looked around in confusion for someone who fit the descriptions the guys had offered.

...Eventually, it seemed to dawn on them that they were the only ones there who fit the profiles.

""" ...?!"""

My friends stood rooted to the spot. Darkness immediately reached behind her head and started playing with her hair, while Megumin began assiduously dusting off her robe.

Aqua spoke up. "You guys, did you just call us beautiful? Did you say we were gorgeous? Say it again!"

....

Nobody in Axel was crazy enough to try to chat up these women. I guess I should've probably complimented them on their appearance every once in a while. I was amazed that they were so amazed.

"Huh? ...Er, we said you were real pretty, and...maybe you'd like to check out the town with us... You know..."

One of the guys spoke on behalf of his crew, all of whom seemed taken aback by Aqua's reaction.

Aqua, Megumin, and Darkness immediately huddled together and started whispering. After a moment, Megumin stepped up as their representative.

"What the three of you are saying, then, is that for the privilege of going out with a staggering beauty like myself and these two other relatively beautiful women, you are prepared to sacrifice coin and life alike, yes? And so won't we date you? That's what you're saying, is it not?"

""""We wouldn't go that far,"""" the three men said.

......!

That was when I had a thought.

Unfortunately…

This country ran on two things: commerce and casinos.

We were eager to see the sights, spread our wings a little.

So what if we joined forces with these three nutjobs?

Think, Kazuma Satou, think!

There was no way these girls wouldn't cause some kind of trouble. And the blame, I was sure, would fall on me. But what if, when the trouble happened, I wasn't there and these three guys were?

....

"Yo… Think we picked some weird ladies?"

"Yeah… Don't you smell trouble? I know we came here for sight-seeing, but I think we might be in over our heads."

"Y-yeah, but even if they are a little weird, they're so hot!"

As the guys held a whispered conference, Aqua and the others came over to me just as I was really getting into my idea. The stupid grins on the girls' faces kind of annoyed me.

"Say, Kazuma, what do you think we should do? I don't knooow, ooh… They called us beautiful. They said they want to go ouuuut with us. You're probably used to being called a loser by now, Kazuma, considering the party you're in. But I hope you understand how grateful you should be to have been able to team up with three breathtaking beauties. Otherwise, we might just drop you like a hot potato and go out with those other guys."

"Please, be my guest."

""""""""Huh?""""""""

The girls weren't the only ones shocked by my reply. The three guys joined the chorus.

"…Ummm, hey, Kazuma? Did you just say…?" Aqua sounded a little anxious.

I knew these girls were all high-level adventurers. I didn't think they would have any trouble with a few random dudes off the street.

Besides, it wasn't up to me to tell them who they could and couldn't go out with.

Now completely convinced that my idea to foist off the girls on these guys was a good one, I answered, "I said, be my guest. What am I, your mom? I want the chance to have some fun, not spend all my time baby-sitting you. No harm in this kind of arrangement from time to time."

""""Huh?!"""""

That really set Aqua and the others back on their heels.

"…Hey, did you hear that guy say something about babysitting them?" one of the men whispered to his friends.

Megumin, starting to look a little desperate, said, "Hold on, Kazuma—this is too sudden! Are you sure about this? Letting me… Letting all of us go play with these boys? Aren't you, you know, jealous, or envious, or—?"

"Not even a little bit."

"You heard him! He said it!"

Megumin seemed really shocked about something, but look. I know we'd been a little bit sweet on each other lately, but it wasn't like we were dating or anything. Though, I guess I wasn't one to talk, given how much I had been going on about Iris recently.

Darkness patted the frozen Megumin on the shoulder. "Hold it, Megumin. We know this guy isn't a straight shooter, right? Heh—he's the classic *tsundere* type!" Then she grinned in my direction like she expected to get a rise out of me. "How about it, Kazuma? Think you can bring yourself to be honest at a moment like this? You're waltzing around town with a bunch of girls so pretty, they get catcalled by random guys on the street. Want to walk arm in arm with me? Maybe I'll trip and my ch-chest will bump into you…"

"Hard pass. I mean, you're ripped. I'll bet your chest is as hard as everything else on you."

"Whaaat?!"

With Darkness standing there totally surprised, the boys started whispering again.

"Geez, what do you make of this guy? He kinda sucks, doesn't he? And I've got a bad feeling about this."

"Yeah, let's back off. We came all the way here to enjoy some sightseeing. We wouldn't want to get caught up in anything *weird*..."

"N-no kidding, no need to put your head in the lion's... Er, so I guess we're giving up...? Man, such hotties, though; total shame... Uh, hey! We just remembered, we've got some stuff to do..."

The guys tried to run away, but I grabbed them. "Didn't you want to date my friends?"

One of them flinched and tried to push my hand away...

...but he couldn't.

"Huh? Ah... Ow, ow-ow-ow...! Sorry! We were just kidding—we're sorry for chatting up your girls! W-we didn't mean any of that 'loser' stuff! We've gotta go now!"

I was an adventurer of a pretty fair level myself. My stats were good enough that I wasn't going to lose a contest of strength to some random street-corner slobs.

"Aw, no, it's fine, for real. My friends here really are good-looking, aren't they? Believe me: I know."

"Uh...huh..."

They looked at me as if they found me suspicious somehow, unable to hide their anxiety. I dropped my voice and whispered to them, "See that blond armored chick there? You oughta see her *without* the armor. Hoo-wee! Those hips!"

The guys swallowed audibly at that. I continued to press my point. "And the lady with blue hair, she loves her some wine. You wanna get in good with her, just say you'll buy her a drink."

The guys looked at one another.

"And the black-haired one... You know the type. Has a cat, loves cute things. Take her somewhere with some nice, cuddly animals; that's my advice."

The guys nodded.

""""Well, okay, if you insist...""""

I stepped away from the newly amenable guys and waved to Aqua and the others.

"Okay, kids, see you later. Have fun spreading your wings today. You can pay me back by not causing trouble for me, starting tomorrow. As for today, knock yourselves out."

""""Huh?"""""

That gave the three guys pause.

Aqua sized them up and said, "Are you ready? I don't have much change on me, so this isn't gonna be cheap. The lovely Aqua only drinks the finest alcohol."

One of the three guys pounded himself on the chest. "D-don't you worry! Money is one thing we've got. Our parents are upper-class, see? We'll cover anything and everything you want to do here in town!"

Bam. There it was.

Now that I had heard, with my own ears, the one thing I really needed to hear, I said, "Awesome, have fun, everyone. I'm gonna go spread my wings someplace else. You guys, I'm trusting you. Don't go running out on my friends and ducking your responsibilities, okay?"

Then I turned around...

"Y-you really never stop surprising me... Somehow I can't abide the way you don't seem to be faking but actually seem to mean what you're saying... It's a bluff, right? Is this all just a bluff? ...You men there, I'm warning you. Don't get any weird ideas about us. Otherwise you never know what the man known as the Devil of Axel Town might do to you."

""""Huh?"""""

I heard Darkness spouting rude nonsense behind me.

"She's right. You see how casually he walks away from his vulnerable, beautiful friends. Surely you can surmise what kind of person he is. If you don't shower us with hospitality, you'll see later just how bad he can be. He may not look like much, but he's broken into a heavily guarded noble household before and can snipe a person from a great distance. If you make an enemy of him, he'll hunt you every moment of every day."

""""!"""""

Hey, stop that.

"Come on, you two; don't be so mean! Kazuma isn't *that* much of a devil. True, he did blow up that governor's house and get charged with sedition, and he did cause enough trouble to get himself banned from the capital, but..."

C'mon, Aqua—try a little harder. I don't think your argument is making sense to them!

""""..........""""

Now the three guys had gone completely quiet as they turned tremblingly toward me...

"...You know, I think we've changed our minds. We'd rather not get inv— Aaahhh! He ran away?!"

One of the guys had been trying to say something.

""""He left! That guy actually went and left!"""""

Aqua, Darkness, and Megumin were shouting something, but I didn't quite hear them. I was too busy disappearing into the streets of Elroad!

2

This was the first foreign country I had visited since coming to this world, and the city was so big, it made me realize that every other place I had visited had been a small town.

And right there, in the middle of Elroad's capital...

"I win again!"

"No waaaaaaaay!"

""""""""Ooooooooooohhh!""""""""""

I had jumped into a card game tournament and was cleaning up.

"Who the hell is this guy?"

"I've never seen him before, but someone has to know a guy this good!"

I could hear the audience murmuring, keeping a respectful distance from my hot streak and me.

"He comes on hard and fast… Doesn't it kind of remind you of what they say about Dark Katrina?"

"You mean the legendary—?! Wait, I heard Dark Katrina is a woman…"

Dark Katrina? Who was that?

"Hold on—look at the way he uses his trap card. Remember Wily Claude?"

"You might be right. Claude's the only one I know who's so nasty with his trap cards…"

And now some Claude guy?

In this world, famous adventurers often acquired a second name. Maybe the same thing happened with famous card sharks. Back in my world, I had been called all sorts of names by the friends I played MMOs with. All-Luck Kazuma, Kill-Steal Kazuma… Okay, so none of them was a *good* name, but still.

…When I came out of my reverie, I found a woman standing before me.

"You're my next victim? Ooh, haven't seen you around before. Looks like you get a lot of good hands, but it takes more than luck to win at this game. Strategy conquers all. You might beat some intermediates with good draws, but it won't help you against a twin-name like me."

I refrained from asking whether her second name was an embarrassing one. Because for the first time in a long time, I was genuinely excited about a game.

"Your winning streak ends here," the girl went on. "With me, Iron Wall Marineth."

Iron Wall Marineth.

The girl, who was obviously older than I was, proclaimed the name without shame, then grinned and drew her cards—!

*   *   *

Everything in town had been new and interesting to me, but my wanderings eventually brought me to this building that occasionally shook with cheers, and I went in to have a look. I observed from the audience for a little while, but when I noticed the card game they were playing bore a lot of similarities to a very famous game I was pretty good at, I jumped right in.

I assumed this game was the work of one of the various Japanese people who had been sent to this world. Knowing it as well as I did (any gamer would have), I bought a standard pack of basic cards and then a premium pack full of sweet rares—the sort of thing that's a fringe benefit of having a ton of money.

Then I built a deck so devilishly powerful, it had been banned in Japan.

"My turn! My turn again! And again and again and again, forever!!"

"He's a monster! I've never seen such brutal combos!"

"There's overkill, and then there's overkill! Just stop already—the game is over!"

"Look, he made Iron Wall Marineth cry. Somebody stop him!"

The shouting from the audience gave me my first gamely satisfaction in a long time.

"Please end it already. I'm sorry for mouthing off to you." My opponent, the young woman, was in tears; the game was over and she hadn't been able to do a single thing.

"Good game. Let's play again sometime."

"Absolutely not. I can't take any more of this."

I reached out for the traditional post-game shake but felt my palm fill with the gentle weight of my winnings.

That's right: This was Elroad, the Casino Kingdom. There wasn't a game around without betting on it.

Fresh off my crushing victory over Marineth, I shouted to the audience:

*   *   *

"I'll take on all challengers!"

A few hours passed. I had kept on winning for a while before leaving the building in high spirits, in search of my next destination. I didn't have anywhere in mind; I was just enjoying exploring an unfamiliar town.

My bulging purse put me in a good mood, but that was when I realized my stomach was growling, so I ducked into a random place…

"Eeeek! Someone, come quick! There's someone who looks like a mummy in the sand bath! Is there anyone here who can use healing magic?!"

I had lunch at a pasta place I found.

"Welcome, welcome, are you by yourself, sir? Have a seat at the counter, please!"

The waitress showed me to the counter and I ordered something at random. While I waited for my food, I took a look around the restaurant, and that was when I overheard some men one table over…

"Aw, man, I made soooo much money today! A toast to Elroad!"

"You got that right. The economy here's so hot, you make money hand over fist no matter what you do. When I heard His Majesty the king was taking an extended trip to another country, I was worried. But that whelp of his sure knows how to run a country!"

"Yeah, and to think we spent all that time calling him Prince Stupid!"

Hmm…?

I'd been told this country was in dire financial straits, so what was this about a red-hot economy? And the "Prince Stupid" thing bothered me, too.

"Maybe, but I hear the good times are all thanks to the prime minister running the government. The idiot prince might have absolute political authority, but I'm told he'd rather play around than rule this place."

"In that case, forget Elroad. A toast to our prime minister!"

""""Yeah, to our great prime minister! Cheers!"""

…This was getting stranger and stranger. So it was the prime minister running the show around here? Did that mean he was the one who had cut off the support to Belzerg? And apparently, the king wasn't even home right now. I was told the prince was about Iris's age. Was it normal in this world for kids that young to take on major political responsibilities? Back when I was Iris's age, I was busy being scolded by my parents for staying up all night playing games…

I put the shop behind me and then, thinking of Iris by herself at our inn, decided to buy her a souvenir. The only thing was, I had no idea what sort of gift would make her happy. I had an inkling that she would act pleased no matter what I got, but it just didn't feel right to get the princess of your nation something too cheap…

"Hey, I heard this awesome entertainer is doing an appearance at Machelin!"

"Machelin? You mean the unbelievably fancy department store? Do they even let entertainers in there?"

"Who cares? Let's check it out! I hear she uses all their expensive merchandise for her tricks!"

Such was the conversation a couple of guys were having as they emerged from a certain small store. I glanced at the sign and saw that the place sold accessories, so I went in to see if there might be anything suitable for a souvenir there.

"'ello," the clerk said without much enthusiasm. He sat behind the counter reading the paper—never even looked up at me.

There was a lot of stuff in there, from handmade girls' necklaces to big bracelets that were probably aimed at men. I glanced over at the counter and saw a glass case holding stuff that looked like it was a cut above the rest of the baubles in the store. Maybe there would be something good in there. I was just searching for something that would look nice on Iris when…

"Wh-whoa! Wh-what's that, an earthquake?!" the clerk exclaimed, accompanied by an intense rattling of the entire establishment. I could hear the sound of an explosion far in the distance, and I felt that I didn't have to think too hard about its origin.

Back when I had snuck into the castle, I had stolen Iris's ring. I still had it, and treasured it for sure, but it would be a little awkward to return it now.

A new ring! That would be perfect!

It was a little ironic, considering I was the one who had stolen the first one, but I was uncomfortable just leaving the poor girl ringless. This would let me return the ring, in a way, even if it was a different one.

And so it was decided. I would get Iris a ring as a souvenir!

I went over to the glass case, hoping to buy the most expensive ring they had, but when I looked inside, I didn't see a single ring.

"Hey, man, don't you sell rings? Expensive ones, ideally?"

"Rings? We don't handle anything that fancy. The only rings we have are the kids' toys over there." The clerk, who had jumped to his feet in surprise at the shaking, pointed to a corner of the store. All that was over there were cheap trinkets for a few hundred eris apiece. Maybe not the sort of thing you should be giving a princess.

Then again, I'd just gotten to this town and had no idea where to get fancy accessories, so what was a man to do?

Wait… That was it.

I would buy one of these, and if I didn't find anything better, then I would give it to Iris.

"Gimme this ring, mister!"

I dropped my new purchase in my pouch and set out again…

3

"Ah, so you're back. And how was your sightseeing?"

It was evening.

The setting was the same place we'd split up that morning.

When I got there, my friends were already waiting for me. Aqua was looking pointedly away from me, while Darkness was blushing contentedly. And as for Megumin, she was getting a piggyback ride from Darkness and looking rather gratified.

As for the three guys who were supposed to be the ladies' escorts...

Well, one was missing. And of the two who were left, one was just sitting there, looking shell-shocked, while the other hugged his knees and shook and mumbled to himself like a textbook trauma patient.

I think I'd be better off not asking...

Megumin took one look at me and seemed to immediately know what I was feeling. "Kazuma, I doubt you want to know, but would you hear us out?"

"...Sure."

I've got no choice...

I casually let my gaze slide over to Darkness, who seemed to be in a great mood.

"...Ahem. Let's begin with the one who isn't here. When he heard we had only just arrived, he suggested we start our day by going to a fancy spa to relieve the stress of travel."

Oh-ho.

Darkness picked up the story: "Wouldn't you know it, when we arrived, it turned out this spa had sand baths, and you know how much I love sand baths. They're a wonderful form of relaxation where you put on an outfit called a *yukata* and lie back and they cover you with warm sand... But that man... I don't know what he was thinking, but he was right behind me. Then he said, *'All riiight, I'm gonna impress sweet li'l Darkness by showing her how long I can stay in this bath!'* And I couldn't resist rising to the challenge..."

"Before we knew it," Megumin said, "the young man had passed out. When the staff noticed, they rushed him to the hospital."

...So that was one down.

Next, I looked at the shaking, muttering guy. Megumin glanced uncomfortably to one side. "...Er, about him. He said he would show us his special place. That place turned out to be a river some ways out of town... And, er, then he says, 'Have a look. It's a famous local tourist spot: the Duxion farm. Aren't they cute?' he says, and shows us a whole flock of Duxions. Well, you know how high in XP Duxions are. They were all bunched up! What could I possibly do but take them all out with an explosion? ...It seems the shock was too much for him..."

He'd been eager to show them a whole flock of Duxions, just to see the lot of them blown to bits before his eyes. I shifted my gaze from the shaking guy to Aqua, who was trying to look as if she had nothing to do with any of this.

...She wasn't doing a very convincing job.

"And, ahem, as for Aqua..." Megumin didn't quite seem to want to say it.

At her words, the paralyzed guy suddenly jumped to his feet. "This lady drinks all the wine at the most expensive place in town, gets totally wasted, and then she goes, 'I'll show you all my amazing tricks!' and starts doing party tricks using the nicest stuff in the store. And I mean, they were awesome tricks. Just killer. But there's got to be a catch! I mean, if you put a handkerchief over a grand piano and make it disappear, it's got to go somewhere, right?! A handkerchief can't even cover a grand piano!"

So she'd been up to her old tricks again, literally and figuratively. They sounded really interesting, though. I would have to have her show me sometime.

"Then I got the bill for the piano and all the other stuff she used in her little show... And then the one for all the Duxions on the farm... I've been begging these people to pay for *something*, even half, but... Ahhh! No, wait, my parents are gonna kill me! Please... Just a third...!"

*   *   *

I put my fingers in my ears and started running in the other direction.

4

"How did you like Elroad? Were you able to spread your wings a bit?" Iris asked when we got back to the inn.

"I've started building my own legend in this town," I said. "And incidentally, these girls are sort of legendary in their own special ways now."

Iris gave me a quizzical look. I guess she didn't get it, but a look at the faces of Darkness and the others told her she was better off not asking.

That same Darkness said, "Well then, Lady Iris, as I'm sure you're much fatigued from all your preparations today, let me suggest you go to bed early so you're ready for tomorrow. I've instructed the servants to bring your food to your room so you can just relax. Please have a pleasant rest and get your strength up."

When had she gotten so polite?

"I think it's still rather early... Er, not that I don't agree that I have to be ready for tomorrow's proceedings." She still looked a little puzzled.

Darkness put on a somewhat theatrical expression of remorse and said, "Lady Iris, you have an immensely important meeting tomorrow. Today of all days, you must not stay up late. You'll need as much rest as you can get so that you will be all the more radiant tomorrow."

"...I see. Okay, I'll go to bed early tonight." She glanced at me but headed to her room.

Darkness immediately clapped her hands. "Excellent! Now, what say we all turn in as well? Big day tomorrow. I know it's a little early, but bodyguards have to rest when they get the chance!"

It was a little strange, but we were tired enough from our trip that at Darkness's urging, we retired to our rooms without giving it much thought...

* * *

I know what's going on here.

This was that thing Darkness had been talking about with Lain: the plan to put me to sleep for a few days. I'd known Darkness long enough that I could see through this little plot of hers.

I went to my room all right, but I sure didn't go to sleep. I was watching. Who knew what she would try to pull? Who knew how she would try to get me to drink her elixir?

The most direct route would be to kick down the door, overpower me, and try to force it down my throat. But there was always a chance I would fight back. I had thought she might try to spike my drink at dinner, but then we all went out to eat. If she was going to make her move, it had to be tonight, but what would it be...?

It happened as I was sitting there trying to read Darkness's mind.

"Kazuma, are you awake?"

There she was, knocking at my door.

It was just past eight o'clock, and even for a world where people tended to go to bed and get up early, it was hardly time to be asleep.

"Sure I am. It's not locked—come on in."

Man, what did she take me for? Did she think I would just roll over and let her give me a sleeping potion? I didn't know what she had in mind, but I would start by taking the initiative and teasing the crap out of—

...At that instant, everything that had been in my mind vanished.

"Oh, uh, okay. I'm coming in, then. I just want to talk a little."

All because of the unbelievably revealing negligee Darkness was wearing.

Darkness came in and set an oversize bottle of alcohol down on the table in the middle of the room.

Looked like I was the one who'd underestimated my opponent. Now I realized: I was dealing with a noble, and they specialized in tricks and ploys. I couldn't believe I had found myself in a honey trap.

"G-g-geez, why are you dressed like that? I can see your, y'know, figure."

"?!"

My interjection sent a flush of embarrassment onto Darkness's cheeks. Good. At least that meant she didn't have it in her to really play the seduction game.

"Oh yeah? This is what I always wear, you know? Besides, people loosen up on the road. But more importantly, um, wanna have a drink?"

She popped the cork on the bottle, managing to keep a straight face despite my barb. There was a neat little *pop!* indicating that the bottle had been sealed until this moment. That meant this couldn't be the spiked drink.

"Fair enough. I guess it is pretty early for bed. I hear a nightcap is good for the health. Don't mind if I do." I took a glass, into which Darkness was about to pour some wine. "Whoa, danger, danger!"

I dropped the glass straight on the floor. It shattered audibly, the pieces scattering everywhere. Darkness paled, but I stuck my hand out toward the pieces. "*Wind Breath!*" My wind magic swept the glass into one corner of the room. "Phew, sorry, Darkness—my hand slipped... Aw, now there's only one glass. I'll get another one from downstairs. We can ask a maid to clean up the broken glass tomorrow."

I made to leave the room...

"W-wait, Kazuma. Look, we, uh, we need just one glass, right? I only ever meant to pour for you. You work so hard all day, I wanted to take care of you for once!"

She had a grip on the hem of my shirt.

For a noble who should have specialized in tricks and plots, she sure was a terrible liar.

"Oh? And how exactly did you want to take care of me? Do I look that tired to you? Me, the guy who sleeps all day?"

"No, I—?! I mean... Uh, we just beat another general of the Demon King the other day! I know we've done that a lot, but it's hard work, isn't it?" Darkness was flustered, trying to come up with some kind of excuse, but she composed herself and looked seriously into my eyes. "I was just thinking, it's all because you brought us together as our party leader. I know we do nothing but cause trouble for you, Kazuma, but I wanted to thank you…"

With that, she gave me a really genuine smile, with no hint of anything behind it. Ah, so that was how nobles operated. They mixed a little truth into their lies.

But I wasn't that naive. I almost caved for a second there, but I'm a serious guy who's careful to doubt everyone he meets.

I gently took Darkness's hand—the one that wasn't holding the bottle of wine.

"I should be thanking *you*. I'm a mere Adventurer, the weakest class. Without you guys, I couldn't do anything at all. You especially, Darkness. If we didn't have you, this party would've been destroyed a dozen times over. I'm the one who should be taking care of you. Here, hand me that bottle. Let me pour for you."

"Wha—?" As I took the hand holding the bottle, Darkness made a sound like she knew I'd seen through her. But when she registered that I was trying to take the drink from her, she said, "N-no, no-no-no. It's okay, Kazuma—your kind words are all I need. And I came here to take care of you tonight. It would be pathetic if I let you do all the work. Here, just let go of that bottle and pick up your glass. I'll get you a drink in no time."

Her voice was calm, but she was struggling to keep me from getting the wine. Judging by her reaction, it was clear now that the drug was already in the glasses.

"Uh-uh, no way. I can't have a distinguished noble like you pouring wine for me. You've got to rest sometimes, young lady, or otherwise— We're going to the castle as bodyguards tomorrow, right? You'll make some awful mistake; I'm sure of it. I can hardly go around acting all informal with you in public!"

Resisting me even more firmly, Darkness finally showed her hand. "Oh, come on—let go! You've never spared one ounce of concern for my well-being. Don't act all deferential now! Hell, you called me *'useless'* just on the way here! Practically every day, you say I'm a worthless woman who can't come through when it counts, but I'll have you know that Crusaders focus on defense, so of course we don't do anything flashy!"

"You let go! I know you didn't have any intention of 'taking care' of me at all tonight, but if you insist on pretending, then I'd be a lot happier with your body than with some wine! There's something funny in this glass; I just know it! If there isn't, then drink from it yourself!"

Neither of us would give in, and it descended into a childish argument.

"Hrk, there's nothing f-funny in there! I swear there isn't, but I'm not going to drink from it. This wine is my special gift to you! I see, so you want my body more than some wine, eh? Fine, if you're so sure, then it's all yours! Get on the bed!"

"Ooh, lashing out at me just so you don't have to admit you were trying to drug me. Real nice! Fine, if you're so sure, then I'll let you take care of me!"

Darkness and I, now that we'd both thrown down the gauntlet, and in a state of high tension, moved over to the bed. I knew that for all her filthy talk, this broad always chickened out when it came down to it. I tore off my shirt and lay spread-eagle on the bed.

"Well, c'mon!"

"D-damn you!"

Darkness looked away, unsure what to do with her eyes now that I was lying there shirtless.

"Ooh, what's the matter? I knew you were all talk, 'young lady'! I figured as much. You always call me incompetent and lazy and whatever else, but you're the one who gets all embarrassed with one little kiss on the cheek!"

"Now you're in for it! Do you think I'm going to just sit here and let some *commoner* treat me like this? I always make good on my promises, so here comes your TLC!"

Almost before she was done talking, Darkness charged at me. But then she didn't seem to know what to do with me lying there.

"Hey, you better not tell me that you had some dumb massage in mind or something! You know what I'm talking about—you and that filthy mind!"

"D-don't you say I have a filthy mind! I'm Lalatina Ford Dustiness. Whatever disadvantage I may be at, I will never run aw—!"

Bam! The door flew open. Megumin was standing there, her eyes flaring red.

"You two have been screaming and shouting for ages now; people are trying to sleep! What in the world are you doing in here?!"

I looked to Megumin for help from my prone position, hoping she would think Darkness had shoved me over. "Help me, Megumin! She's trying to jump me!"

"D-damn you—!"

5

"I can't fathom what you are thinking, Darkness. I will not say you should abandon all desire, but Iris is staying with us here, remember? At least save these antics for after we get home."

"No, Megumin, it's not like that! I can explain!"

After Megumin came bursting into our room, I had tattled on Darkness to save myself.

"What do you mean, 'it's not like that'? You tried to drug me. There's a sleeping potion or something in that glass, right? No? Then take a sip of that wine out of the glass you brought. I know you must have been planning to have your way with me after you drugged me to sleep. You've got a record."

"N-n-n-n-no, I wasn't going to—! I swear there's a good reason…"

With the incontrovertible evidence sitting right there, Darkness was going to have trouble getting out of this one. And there was one more bit of proof.

"How can you keep saying that when you're dressed in such a lewd outfit? You're one light breeze away from a wardrobe malfunction! So nothing you say will convince me! Come on—own up!"

That's right. The unusually salacious negligee she was wearing had come back to haunt her. Megumin wasn't the only one who wanted to know what she had been thinking to dress like that; I wanted to find out, too.

"This dress! …Ugh… I—I was planning to drug Kazuma to sleep so he couldn't do anything unpleasant during tomorrow's meeting, but I ended up feeling a little bad making him miss out on a country full of entertainment…"

"I see, and so you dressed like that so he could at least enjoy himself a bit before he blacked out. And no doubt you were hoping a little something might come of it, as well…! Argh, what a reprehensible noblewoman you are!"

Megumin had drawn her line in the sand, and Darkness finally looked resigned. "No, I…! Oh… Urgh… I won't deny it anymore. I am a terrible noble…"

"You truly are. If your dear father back in Axel heard you were up to such doings, what would he say? *Hff, hff…* Come now—speak clearly!"

Megumin was really laying into Darkness. Sometimes I wondered if she actually had a bit of a bully streak…

Still lacking my shirt, I sat cross-legged in front of Darkness and savored the moment as she was forced to sit formally on the bed. "Gosh, I can't believe you. I'm not so stupid that I would do anything that isn't for Iris's benefit, okay? I'm not going to suddenly attack her fiancé or whatever, so relax. I just hate to see someone married off when they don't want to be. When you were about to be forced into tying the knot with that lord, I rescued you, right?"

"………"

Maybe Darkness was thinking about the time I had come to help her, because her ears flushed a little.

"If this is really what Iris wants, then I have no intention of getting in the way. What I don't want is for someone to force themselves into a match they aren't interested in, just to sacrifice themselves. Especially not when it's someone I know. It kind of bugs me to see a female friend of mine go to another guy, even if she isn't someone I want to date or whatever."

"That's quite a pronouncement, coming from the man who abandoned us to three strangers this very afternoon."

"She's right. I'd love to see what's going on in that dense head of yours."

"That was because I trusted you. You girls aren't so easy that you'd go running off with some random guys who picked you up on the street, are you?"

The faces of Megumin and Darkness flashed with conflicted emotions, and they looked at each other uncomfortably.

"This man can be quite beyond the pale at times. What a thing to say, when he does whatever he feels like."

"Absolutely. For someone who looks like he'd run off with any pretty thing on two legs, he's got a lot of nerve…"

Geez, sounds like they don't trust me at all.

Though to be fair, while I was off on my own that afternoon, I *did* check to see if there were any good, shady shops like a branch of the succubus-service palace.

Darkness got to her feet with a touch of exasperation. "Fine. I won't say another word. I guess I don't really have the right, seeing as I've turned down matches myself so often. If anything happens, I'll take responsibility, so you do whatever you want. My house and I will back you up."

"I like the sound of that. Hey, that lady Claire said the same thing. With two big noble houses behind me, I can cut loose a little."

When I showed her the signet pendant, Darkness exclaimed in surprise, "Lady Claire entrusted something like that to someone like you?! Do you even know what that is?!"

"No clue, but judging by your reaction, at least I can guess that white-suited lady trusts me more than you do."

Maybe Darkness was chagrined to hear that, considering she had known me so much longer than Claire had, because she took a similar pendant from around her neck…

"Kazuma, because I do trust you, I'm g…ugh, uuugh…g-giving you this…"

"Aw, what? If you're gonna give it to me, then skip the drama and hand it over! C'mon—leggo!" She didn't actually hold the pendant out to me, so I pried it from her hand and put it around my own neck. "Anyway, leave tomorrow to me. The main thing is to keep these goons happy enough that the defense money continues to flow, right? I won't mess that up. You know I wouldn't do anything to make Iris unhappy, don't you?"

"I see… Yes, of course. I understand. I'll let you handle everything. Take care of Lady Iris for us! And if everything goes smoothly…" Darkness looked at me with genuine relief. "This time, I won't just give you some kiddie kiss on the cheek. I'll make sure it's more adult…"

She trailed off so much at the end that I could barely hear her, but thanks to my lip-reading ability, I knew exactly what she had said.

And believe me, I would hold her to it.

6

"Hoo-wee. That is one expensive-looking building. Darkness, I think their capital has our capital beat, at least on economy and castle size."

The next morning.

When we arrived at Elroad's castle, we were floored by how large and elaborate it was.

"I shall not stand for this. I wonder how it would hold up if hit with explosion magic. The mere thought makes me want to recite my incantation."

"…Right, Megumin, we'll take things from here, so you just head back to the inn." Darkness was quick to rein in the jabbering Megumin.

"Hey, hey, imagine how surprised everyone would be if I showed off my trick. I could change the symbol on that flag up at the tippy top there to an Axis Church one."

"Aqua, Aqua. Listen, when we get back to Axel, I'll have the Dustiness family make a big donation to the Axis Church if you just behave yourself today." Darkness looked like she might burst into tears trying to restrain Aqua, who was gazing up at the top of the castle.

Sheesh. Every member of this party was a problem child, and she had focused all her attention on me. "All riiiight, time to put this punk to the test. I wonder how long he'll last."

"What happened to everything you said last night?! If you're going to be making up harebrained schemes, then give me back my pendant— Huh?!"

Darkness made a swipe for the pendant around my neck, but I dodged her and nimbly hid it away.

"Wh-where are you putting my family's pendant?" she demanded. "That thing is like a treasure to us…!"

I guess she didn't like where I had hidden the pendant, because Darkness was on the attack. "Hey, keep it down. Where do you think we are? We may be bodyguards, but we're representing our country, too. Show a little respect," I told her.

"*You're* telling *me* about respect? Ugh, please, please behave yourself…!"

Iris, watching us yell at each other, giggled. "This will be the first time I'll be meeting my prince, but I'm not nervous, since I've got all of you here. Thank you so much."

"See? Iris is cool as a cucumber. So why's her adviser the noisiest one in the room?"

"Whyyy, y-y-youuu…! And just whose fault is it that I'm so upset…?!"

It had been twenty or thirty minutes since we'd been told to stop and wait in front of the castle, where the owner himself, the prince, would come out to meet us. We were teasing Darkness partly because we were tired of waiting, but at that moment…

*   *   *

"Geez, that's a bunch of Belzerg bumpkins for you… Yapping and shouting right in front of a castle. Learn how to act, for crying out loud."

…there came the distinctly crackly voice of an adolescent boy. The kid looked to be about Iris's age. He was surprisingly tall for how young he was—almost as tall as I was. He had red hair and was surrounded by a huge entourage of advisers and supporters, as if trying to show off how powerful he was. The tiny crown resting on his head clued me in that this was Iris's fiancé.

"Do you see that, Darkness? Your inability to be calm and mature has gotten us scolded."

"My goodness, Darkness. We're dealing with royalty, remember? This is no place for your yelling."

"Grrrrr…!"

Megumin and Aqua gave Darkness a taste of her own medicine, and she lowered her head and flushed with embarrassment.

"Um…" Until that moment, Iris had stayed behind Darkness, but now she emerged in front of her senseless, indecorous companion. "Would you be Lord Levy, the first prince of Elroad? I am the first princess of Belzerg, Iris. I've come to this country to parley with you. It's a pleasure to make your acquaintance."

She smiled with complete, sincere innocence, speaking in a pleasant voice that was neither too loud nor too soft. She executed a perfect bow, practically oozing elegance and loveliness. Standing there proudly as if to cover for Darkness, there was no hint of the timid, retiring girl I'd seen at our first meeting—just the rightful princess of an entire nation.

"L-Lady Iris…!" Darkness said, clearly moved to see her ruler, the girl she had thought of almost like a little sister, show such brilliance. I knew I wasn't one to talk, but it seemed like Claire and Darkness were both pretty overprotective of Iris.

"So you're my betrothed, eh? I thought Belzerg's royal girls were supposed to be able to kick as much butt as their boys, but you don't look so tough. I was picturing someone stronger, someone more awesome. Boo."

"Wha—? Oh, I... Pardon me..."

Hmm?

"And what's this? Four bodyguards? Can't Belzerg afford more than that? I'm sure you're all real strong or whatever, but you need to learn how to save some money!"

Then Prince Levy gave a nasty chuckle, causing his small entourage to laugh approvingly.

Ugh, what a little snot. I couldn't believe this was how he chose to make a first impression. Prince? He was just a dumb kid. I didn't think much of his retainers, either. Heck, what had happened to our countries being friends or allies or whatever? They sure didn't act like it.

...Then Prince Levy's interest seemed to turn from Iris to those of us standing with her. The people behind him did the same, turning their condescending gazes from Iris to us. When they saw Aqua and Megumin, several pairs of eyes went wide with surprise.

Levy, though, didn't notice; he went right on mocking us. "And those bodyguards, don't get me started. All so young, and not a decent piece of equipment on them. I can't believe you survived the trip."

This time, there was no chorus of laughter to back him up. Surprised, the prince turned around.

"I believe I shall take you up on that challenge," Megumin said, stepping forward with her crimson eyes flashing.

7

Maybe this kid thought he was being diplomatic. I didn't get his logic, but the prince obviously intended to bait us, to try to get a rise out of us. But there was one thing he hadn't counted on...

*   *   *

"Please don't! Prince Levy knows but little of your nation and was unaware of the existence of the Crimson Magic Clan! Despite his provocations, he wasn't seriously challenging you…!"

"My prince, please take a close look at our visitors! That is a member of the Crimson Magic Clan, a group so dangerous that even the Demon King fears them. They are not known for their sense of humor, so please be careful not to say anything careless to her!"

"Y-yeah, okay, I'm sorry! It was my bad! Just please stop chanting your spell!"

At the desperate urging of his retainers, the prince, looking spooked, apologized to Megumin.

"I will overlook your behavior this one time, but next time I shall not be so forgiving, eh? My name is Megumin. Master of Explosion and slayer of many generals of the Demon King. You had best not raise my ire."

"We understand that very well now, Lady Megumin. Rest assured. We will see to it that no such offense be committed in the future!" One of the retainers was apologizing profusely, but the prince himself still looked a bit peeved.

Beside me, Darkness was rubbing her temples with both hands, looking close to tears.

"I don't really get it, but at least I'm glad you know how to apologize. When I heard you say we bodyguards didn't look like much, I had half a mind to smite you with a holy boom, but I'll forgive you, too, this time."

Just when it looked like we could let the whole matter slide, Aqua had to butt in with her usual brand of stupidity. The prince looked at her, annoyed. "You, a priest, dare speak that way to me, a—?"

"Prince! My prince! This is a follower of the Axis Church. And the blue color of her hair suggests she is quite devout! Followers of this church are more dangerous than a Leisure Girl, harder to shake off than the undead!" One of the prince's retainers whispered a very well-warranted warning just as the boy was about to switch his target to Aqua.

"Excuse me, but I'd appreciate it if you wouldn't talk about the Axis Church like we are friends with Leisure Girls and undead! Apologize for talking about my sweet lambs as if they are monsters!"

Aqua was a monster, all right—a monster complainer. The prince, thoroughly cowed, turned a nervous look on Darkness and me. The whispering with his attendant continued.

"So let me guess—Blondie there is something special, too?"

"The young woman you see there is the noble Lady Dustiness. Hailing from a noble family known as the King's Shield, she comes from a long line of powerful knights. I can't recommend making an enemy of her…"

They weren't trying to hide their mouths, so Read Lips made their conversation as clear as day to me.

Then, naturally, the prince's gaze fell on me…

"And what about the pathetic-looking guy…?"

"Hmm, I've never seen or heard of him. I assumed he was just along to carry their bags."

Oh, they were gonna pay.

Just when we were all struggling for a way to wrap things up…

"What is all this commotion about?"

A man emerged from the castle. He seemed perfectly ordinary, but one glance at his elaborate clothing made it obvious he was a bigwig around here. He looked more dignified than the prince as he walked forward, almost seeming to float.

"My Lord Prime Minister!" one of the retainers said. "Ahem, you see…"

Well, that explained who he was anyway. He must be the guy people had been gossiping about in the restaurant the day before: the prime minister leading the country by the nose.

As everyone else hurried to suck up to him, Iris composed herself and said, "Greetings. I am Iris, First Princess of Belzerg. It is an honor to meet you."

"Well now, this here is far cuter than anything I expected to see from the royal family of Belzerg. I am Lugkraft, humbly serving as prime minister. I look forward to a productive meeting with you."

All the chatter had died down the moment the prime minister appeared. He greeted the rest of us solicitously, then turned and started walking away. We heaved a collective sigh of relief and followed him.

"If you will, Lady Iris, you and your company may follow me. Preparations for your reception have commenced…" At that exact moment, Aqua wandered up to the man and gave him a nonchalant pat on the back. "Y-yes, priest? Can I help you in some way?"

Aqua cocked her head. "I don't quite know why, but you sort of bug me, mister. You don't have the stink of a demon, and you don't feel like an undead… Hey, mister, you wouldn't happen to be consorting with demons, right? Or keeping a feral undead as a pet, maybe?"

Darkness immediately started bowing and trying to cover. "I'm so sorry, Lord Lugkraft! This person is a follower of the Axis Church—a group of known crazies!"

That caused Aqua to try to slip away from the hand Darkness was using to restrain her.

"Ah, well, an Axis follower can hardly be blamed for acting irrationally. Please don't worry. It truly doesn't bother me…"

But ever since Aqua had touched him, the prime minister's expression had been strained.

8

"I—I beg your assistance in this matter!"

Iris, who had been conferring with the prime minister, spoke in a voice that could be heard all throughout the audience chamber.

Just as the prime minister had told us, we found ourselves welcomed when we entered the castle. For a party in a big, economically powerful country, the reception seemed weirdly low-key.

"Your begging may be for naught, I'm afraid. Our nation is up against a financial wall. Just look at this party. We are welcoming the princess of Belzerg, our cherished ally, and yet, this is the most lavish reception we can afford. Thus, you see, even at your personal request, Lady Iris, we cannot hope to take on any more of the financial burden of defense."

The prime minister looked suitably apologetic, but his refusal was adamant. Us, the prime minister, the prince, and his entourage were the only ones at the table in the little reception hall, although we were stuffing our faces.

"But from what I've seen so far, I cannot say this looks like a nation on the brink of financial collapse…," Iris said. I was hanging around as inconspicuously as I could, and it sounded like they were getting to the heart of the matter.

"I grant, it may appear so to an outsider. But those who live in this country are in extreme duress, by no means able to offer support…"

"I—I see…" Iris drooped at that.

Normally, I would have expected Darkness, our resident noble, to say something. Unfortunately, she was too busy glaring at our two problem children, who were eating and drinking everything in sight.

Well, I would simply have to pick up the slack.

"'Scuse me. Mind if I butt in?"

"E-Elder Brother?"

I inserted myself between the chatting parties, provoking a not-so-subtle look of disgust from the minister.

"You're one of Lady Iris's bodyguards, as I recall. The lady and I are currently engaged in a discussion of great gravity. Perhaps whatever you have to say could wait until later?"

"Nah, don't worry about it—I'm this kid's big brother. Think of me like her guardian."

The prime minister stared at me incredulously, especially when I said "big brother." The toadies in the hall picked up the refrain: "Big brother? That's Prince Jatice?!"

"I see... Yes, Lady Iris did call you Elder Brother, but I never imagined... The last I heard, you were on the front lines, fighting the Demon King. Perhaps I was misinformed. And that black hair and those black eyes... Could they have been passed down to you from the Hero?"

The prime minister busied himself mistaking my identity. I didn't know what he was going on about, with all this muttering about black hair, black eyes, and inheriting things from ancestors, but this was obviously my chance.

"Regardless," he concluded, "the august nature of the person issuing the request makes no difference, I'm afraid. We cannot spare anything for further support. I am terribly sorry, but I'm going to have to ask you to resign yourselves to that fact." He sounded especially emphatic, like he was a little worried about me.

I should've known we weren't going to get anything out of the prime minister. But that still left... "I see, I see... Iris, in that case, let's go ask Prince Levy. I assume you have no objections if the prince himself says he'll give us the money?"

"What?! Of course I would object! I've been telling you we simply don't have the means! And on top of that, *I* run the government in this country, so no matter what the prince says..."

Cracking my knuckles, I leaned in nice and close to the livid prime minister. "A little birdie in town told me that the prince has final authority over every political decision. People seemed to have a lot of good things to say about you, too, Prime Minister. Like how the country was rolling in cash thanks to you. But what's this—good times? Well, that doesn't sound like what you've been telling us, does it?"

In a voice that made him sound like he was passing a kidney stone, the prime minister said, "Very well. Only, you must conduct your negotiations with the prince by yourselves. As for me, I have no authority to intercede."

It sounded like he was washing his hands of the matter. That was fine by me. This prince didn't look like the sharpest knife in the drawer anyway.

Iris and I trotted over to the prince, the prime minister following as if to keep an eye on things. I guess he wanted to make sure the kid didn't get sucked in by whatever we said.

Iris smiled at the prince, who was engaged in conversation with one of his attendants. "How are you this day, Prince Levy? Might I be so bold as to speak with you for a moment?"

The prince, who had been chatting happily, instantly took on a sore look. "I was fine until about five seconds ago. What would you want to talk about? I don't have anything to say to some barbarian princess from Belzerg."

The venom just kept coming...

That does it. I'm gonna strangle this runt.

"Hey, punk, you've got some nerve speaking to my little sister like that. What, never heard of being polite? You making fun of us? Pretty trash fiancé if you ask me."

"E-Elder Brother!"

"Huh?! How dare you, you dumb, ugly... Elder Brother?"

Iris grabbed me by the arm and dragged me to a corner of the room. "Elder Brother, *please*. Please don't let your temper get the better of you. Our nation desperately needs defense money as well as funds to go on the offensive. Otherwise, we won't even be able to pay rewards to adventurers. Please, for my sake, bear with him, will you?"

Looking into Iris's beseeching eyes, I pushed down my boiling anger. "...I guess I can't say no when you put it that way."

As for the prince, he was holding a whispered conference with his prime minister and entourage. I assumed they were explaining to him who I was. Or at least, who they thought I was.

"Phew, look, sorry about that. Having your little sister mocked right in front of you just strikes a nerve, y'know? I mean, it was kind of your own fault, but we're willing to let bygones be bygones. I was *this* close to siccing my crazy Crimson Magic Clan member and nutjob Axis follower on you."

"Hrk?! U-um, yeah. I went a little too far myself. Let's just say it's water under the bridge."

What a delightful reaction. I guess he knew enough to be afraid of the Crimson Magic Clan and the Axis Church.

This was a good chance to ask him about the money. Iris seemed to pick up on what I was thinking, because she gave me a little nod and looked at the prince. "In fact, Your Majesty, we wished to speak to you regarding the matter of money for the defense…"

Iris had hardly finished speaking before the prince said, "Impossible." There was no sign of the cowering boy from an instant ago; suddenly, he carried himself like a prince. "Lugkraft's given me the details. There can only be, and has only ever been, one answer, and that's absolutely not."

So this was what it meant to find yourself adrift and helpless.

"Er, if I may ask, why not? Without your support, Belzerg will be overrun by the Demon King, and once he has conquered us, Elroad will be his next target."

"Oh, you don't need to worry about that. I've already got it covered. Our nation doesn't plan to resist the Demon King. So I can hardly go around handing out money to fight him."

…

"What…? Wh-what do you mean, Your Majesty? What's to become of the alliance between our nations?"

"Eh, we have our own stuff to deal with. If you want to continue the alliance, fine, but the main thing is not to aggravate the Demon King and his army. Oh, and you can go ahead and consider the engagement annulled if you want. It was really my parents' idea anyway. I never wanted to get married to some barbarian princess from stupid Belzerg. What self-respecting guy would marry a girl who was stronger than he was?"

One second.

That's approximately how long I thought I saw a happy look pass over Iris's face, but then she dissolved into tears and grabbed the prince by the chest with both hands. "I don't care one bit if you call off our engagement. But without that money...!"

"Get as angry as you want—I don't care. If you're half the royal you say you are... Glrgh. W-wait, stop, I can't br—! Stop, hold on...!"

Iris's hands were around his collar now, the prince's face turning white before our very eyes. His attendants were in an uproar.

"*Cough, hack!* Geez, you really are a barbarian!" the prince declared, his own eyes brimming now. "I was right not to marry you! If you're all done talking, then get the hell out of here!"

"...Very well," Iris said, her head drooping.

The prince grinned. "Yeah? Then—"

"I shall return tomorrow," she announced before he could finish.

"...Huh?" That caught him off guard.

Iris puffed out her little chest proudly. "I shall speak to you again tomorrow. And not only tomorrow. The day after that, as well, and the day after that. I shall speak to you until you agree to support us."

The prince's jaw fell open as Iris stared him down. "W-well, just you try!" he said, collecting himself.

Iris grinned from ear to ear when she heard that. "Yes, Your Majesty, I certainly will!"

And with that, she took my hand and spun on her heel.

The prince shouted from behind us. "Hey, starting tomorrow, you only get one bodyguard! Don't bring your Crimson Magic whatevers or your Axis so-and-sos! And leave that Dustiness girl home, too! Just that wimpy-looking brother of yours!"

It was all the resistance he could offer.

Chapter 4

Praise for This Martial Princess!

1

The next morning. Iris and I were seeing everyone off in front of the inn.

"'Kay, then, Kazuma, we'll see you later. I'm gonna win today; I can feel it. When I had my tea, there was a stalk floating upright in it, and that's good luck!"

"I saw you, Aqua. You just kept pouring cups for yourself until you got a lucky stalk in one of them."

Aqua was headed to the casino. Megumin was going off on her own; she said there was a place she wanted to find.

"Kazuma, I'm trusting you with Lady Iris. Much as it irks me, the prince explicitly told me to stay away, so I guess I have to. I'm going to look around town and see if I can find something we can use as leverage."

With that, Darkness also headed into town. And then—

"We will be going as well, then. I swear we'll get that support money!"

Iris and I were going to the castle first thing in the morning to make good on yesterday's promise.

Darkness beckoned me over. "I'm sorry you have to deal with this, Kazuma. Normally, this sort of thing would be my job, but..."

"Don't worry; I'll take care of it. I told you, I won't let anyone make Iris unhappy."

Darkness nodded seriously at me.

"I'll be at the casino, kids. If I hit the jackpot, I'll buy you a souvenir, Kazuma!"

Aqua's remark was like a signal that sent us in our different directions.

The prince had a little surprise in store for us when we got to the castle.

"I'm sorry, but what do you mean, *'en garde'*…?"

We had been ushered onto a training ground.

"Why so shocked? As far as I'm concerned, our negotiations ended yesterday. You insist on continuing them, but I don't see the point." Then he gestured toward the knights in the training area. "I do, however, love a good melee. If you can beat all my minions here, I'll hear you out. Fair?"

"I accept!" Iris said immediately. Then she drew her sword as if it was the most natural thing in the world and stood in front of the prince with a big smile on her face.

I was supposed to be the bodyguard around here, but apparently, Iris meant to handle this herself. The knights, not expecting this slip of a girl to take up the prince's challenge, looked startled for just a second, then…

"Prince Levy, please let me handle this!"

"No, let me! I'll teach this smart-mouthed little girl some respect."

"Hold on. I'm the weakest member of this brigade. It only makes sense that I should be her first opponent…"

The knights, miffed by what they saw as mockery from us outsiders, stumbled over themselves to get in the ring.

The prince smiled indulgently. "Hold your horses, guys… Say, you sure you're going to be okay? Not going to have your big brother handle this?" He smirked at Iris.

Iris casually lowered her blade and said, "Don't worry about me. Elder Brother need not dirty his hands with this affair; I will be more than enough to handle it. Well, everyone? Come at me!"

That was beyond what the knights could take. She *had* said "everyone." And so...

"Not even one-on-one? I know Belzerg is famous for fighting strength, but I think you underestimate us, Princess." A man who looked like the knights' captain spoke to Iris, practically oozing killing intent.

"I certainly don't mean to insult you, but... Well, I *will* take on any number of you at once, and I am prepared to do so at any time."

The guy took the bait, and without even waiting for a signal to start, he raised his sword—

"*Exterion*!"

Iris's almost casual swipe knocked it clean out of his hands.

"...Buh?"

Gee, who said that?

The laughing, raging knights were stone-still now; you could have heard a pin drop on the training grounds.

"Iris," I said, "if you ruin all their swords, this place won't be much good for training, will it? Here, there's a dull training blade over there. Use that one."

"Oh! You're absolutely right; I'm so sorry... I'm sorry. I didn't mean to destroy your sword." She looked genuinely apologetic.

"What?!" said the guy whose sword she had cut in half. "N-no, uh... Please, don't bother your royal self about it...?"

He still didn't seem to know quite what had happened.

Everyone watched, troubled, as Iris pattered over to the wall and grabbed the blunt sword.

"Very well, everyone, you may commence!"

Her smile covered her whole face.

"Um... C-could we speak to you now...?"

"Yes. By all means."

The training area was strewn with battered knights. In the middle of it all sat the prince, as meek as a kitten.

Iris, who didn't have a drop of sweat on her brow despite the immense violence she had just inflicted, drove the training sword into the dust of the floor and smiled at the prince. "Thank you very much! In that case…"

"Wait! I've told you I'll hear what you have to say, but I'm not promising support! Don't get ahead of yourself!"

Sure. Like a kid who loses a game of rock, paper, scissors and then says it's best of three.

"Hey, Iris, all his knights are knocked out at the moment. No witnesses. I think this would be a great time to bury this little brat and go home."

"Hrk?!"

"N-no, Elder Brother, we mustn't! Then we wouldn't get the money!"

Iris objected, not on moral grounds but because we wouldn't get paid. My sweet little sister was growing up.

"…One-tenth," the prince said, almost in a groan.

"Wha—?" Iris asked, looking at him.

"One-tenth! For starters. A-ahem, you're not wrong that having the defense funds suddenly dry up entirely would be problematic. We'll continue providing one-tenth of the previous amount!"

"G-good heavens! With that little, we would hardly be able to…"

Iris was clearly distressed; the prince finally got a chance to wear a triumphant grin. "Well, you did put on a pretty good show for me…for a country bumpkin. Think of this as my way of thanking you! You want more cash? Then show me another good time!"

"Very well! Please bring in the next group of knights, then!"

The prince hadn't expected this and was quick to walk it back. "Okay, no. You're not gonna just keep beating up my soldiers! I said show *me* a good time!"

"A good time… V-very well, erm, you may borrow my treasured bamboo dragonfly for one day…"

"Are you makin' fun of me?! That's just a kids' toy; that's not what

I'm talking about!" The prince growled at Iris, thoroughly worked up. "Tomorrow! Come back here tomorrow. I'll have an opponent ready for you who'll knock your socks off. If you win again, then I might see my way to a little more cash for you. Got it?"

Then he took his leave.

We left the castle and headed back to rejoin the others.

Iris, looking glumly at the ground, mumbled, "Elder Brother, I was only able to recover one-tenth of our support…"

We had come here originally hoping to not only continue to get money for defense but to ask them for something extra for an attack. It was understandably depressing to have our budget slashed instead.

"Don't worry about it. One day, one tenth. Just keep going back every day, and in twenty days of threatening—er, talking with him, we'll have twice what we started with. That'd be a big success, don't you think?"

I was trying to cheer her up, and it worked: Iris looked at me, a smile blooming on her face. "I can't help thinking it's not going to be that easy, but I do feel better. Elder Brother, I hope I can count on you for tomorrow."

"You sure can. Just so you know, I plan to actually do something tomorrow."

That was how our days of negotiating began…

2

"*Exterion!*"

"Y-y-y-you're kidding, right?!" The shout echoed around the training room. It came, of course, from the prince.

"Heh! Looks like you misjudged my little sister's power. Believe me, no griffin is a match for Iris."

"Y-you're the one who got all upset, saying a caged griffin was cruel and unusual and against the rules!"

Lying before us at that moment was the body of the griffin, cut clean in half by a single blow.

A griffin. A monster the size of a house, who had wings and could fly and sometimes even made off with horses or cattle: body of a lion, head of an eagle. It was no dragon, sure, but it was still the sort of dangerous enemy that instilled fear in the hearts of most adventurers.

"Elder Brother, I did it!"

"Y-you sure did. That's my little sister… Nice work."

Iris wandered over to me with a big smile on her face, and I answered with only a little hesitation.

"Um, Prince Levy. So now you'll…"

"Y-yeah, yeah, fine! I'll give you more money, so put your sword away! Don't point that thing at me!"

He was nearly in tears. Iris let out a sigh of relief. Her smile disappeared, though, at what the prince said next.

"But not much more. Between yesterday and today, I'm willing to give you fifteen percent of the support money. All right, now show yourselves out…"

"Impossible! At least make it twenty percent!"

"I s-said not to point that thing at me… Yikes, stay back! Your sword is touching my cheek! A-are you trying to threaten me?!"

I couldn't blame Iris for unwittingly stalking closer to him with her sword.

"Threaten you? No, no, I'm only negotiating…"

"Then *put the sword away!*" the prince wailed, but in spite of this display, he was enough of a ruler that the "threat" didn't work on him. I'd assumed he was a nasty little twerp, but maybe he actually had some guts.

Still, he constantly looked down on us as bumpkins. In that case…

"How about a contest with me, then?"

We had to wound his pride—that's it.

"Wh-why would I want to have anything to do with you?"

"Now, now, don't get the wrong idea, okay? I've done in a laundry list of the Demon King's generals. And seeing as your knights and your griffin couldn't even beat my little sister... Heh, I guess maybe if you brought in a dragon..."

Having had his bluff called, the prince gulped audibly, but Iris, who knew exactly how strong I was (or wasn't), was looking at me like I was crazy.

Please stop gawking at me like that. My heart can't take it.

"What I'm proposing is: Let's play a game. You run a whole country of casinos. So you must be a betting man—am I right?"

Last night, after I got back to the inn, Darkness had told me everything she'd learned about the prince that day. According to her, this kid adored gambling and games of chance. It only made sense. Elroad was built on casinos, after all.

"You want to challenge me in a game? And I suppose if you win, you plan to ask for more money?"

"Yeah, pretty much. You know about doubling down, right? Going double on the stakes after you win a bet? That's what I'm suggesting for you and me."

I'll give the prince a bit more credit. He was quick. He picked up on what I was doing right away.

Darkness's information said he hated to lose. She might not be much use in battle, but for little daily tasks like this, she was surprisingly useful.

Incidentally, as for the other two, one of them had wasted all her allowance at the casino, while the other went back to the Duxion farm and used some cash Darkness lent her to hunt the remaining monsters. She was pretty pleased about it.

I didn't expect either of them to be much use in the immediate future, so I let it ride.

The prince thought for only a moment before he nodded. "All right, if I lose, I'll boost you up to twenty percent. And if you lose, what will you give me?"

Crap, I hadn't thought about my bet. If an entire nation was asking for money, it wasn't going to be pocket change. I had to come up with something just as valuable…

"Okay, I've got it. If you win, my little sister will give you a shoulder rub."

"I'll do my best, Elder Brother!"

"How stupid are you?! No one would want that! Money talks, 'Elder Brother'! Pony up some cash or at least offer me something valuable!"

I didn't have cash; that was why I was resorting to this.

Iris hesitantly took something out of her pocket. "Um, in that case, if we should lose, I would lend you my flying spinner for three days…"

"I told you, I don't care about some dumb toy!"

That looked like the flying spinner I'd given her ages ago. I guess it still meant a lot to her.

"How about this: When you do lose, you get *zero* support money. Not a little less or whatever, just nothing. I'm only entertaining you here because you supposedly came to negotiate, so surely you can agree to that. I assume you'll be coming back every day, so fine: No matter how much money you pry out of me, if you lose even once, it's all gone. Still up to the task?" He smirked tauntingly at us.

Ah… So if we lost even one time, he would take all our money away.

Pretty good move on his part.

Or it would have been, if his opponents hadn't been Iris and me.

"Okay, sounds good to me," I said. "I'll set the terms of the contest, then."

The prince looked totally startled; maybe he hadn't expected me to accept so quickly. As he watched, I took a single coin from my purse. I put both hands behind my back, then presented the prince with my two closed fists.

"The game couldn't be simpler. Guess where the hundred eris coin is."

"…You're betting everything on the most straightforward gamble in the world? Seriously, are you an idiot? You know you can't take this back, right?"

He looked at me with outright pity, but this time Iris spoke up. "I get it, Elder Brother! You have incredibly good Luck! So we might just…!"

"…What?" That brought a bead of sweat to the prince's forehead. But, recognizing that he couldn't back out now, he stared at my fists for a long moment, and then…!

"This one… No, this one! It's in this hand!" he said, pointing to my right fist.

Iris brought her hands together as if she was praying.

The prince's eyes widened when he saw the smirk on my face.

"Buzz! Too bad!"

"Daaaammmmiiiiittt!"

I made a show of opening my hand to reveal nothing inside.

"Well done, Elder Brother! Now we get twenty percent! Twenty!"

Iris was so innocently happy. But the prince, to our surprise, smiled as if he wasn't bothered. "Don't get too pleased over one little victory, okay? Unlike you two, I only have to win one single time. Brace yourselves for tomorrow!"

3

"*Sacred Lightning Flare*!!"

A bolt of bright lightning slammed down in the center of the training field. It dispersed in a blinding flash, kicking up a violent wind.

""Yeeeeek?!"" the prince and I exclaimed, covering our heads.

When the roaring stopped, there was a pile of rubble there. This was the sort of spell the Hero would use against the last boss.

"Elder Brother, I did it!"

The perpetrator of this terrifying phenomenon approached me with a broad smile on her face.

This time, Iris had been facing a crowd of golems. The prince, having decided that even the biggest, baddest opponent he could find would be helpless one-on-one, had switched to mob tactics, but...

"Great work! That's my little sister. What do you think, Your Majesty? How about you stop all this nonsense and go back to helping us?"

"I saw you—you were covering your head and screaming just like I was. But in any event, if you want my support money, you'll have to keep beating me. Right now, you're up to twenty-five percent. What do you say? Got the guts to challenge me for another day?"

The prince kept smirking, but I wordlessly showed him a coin.

"Huh, some nerve! I don't know how good your Luck is, but I'm the prince of a country that makes all its money from casinos. How long do you think you can keep beating the house?"

I didn't say anything, just flipped the coin in the air. I snatched it as it came down and put my hands behind my back...

"...So long story short, we're up to thirty percent. At this rate, we'll have the funding back to normal by the end of the week."

"...Geez, I don't know whether to be impressed or what. Who knew that outrageous Luck of yours would save the world one day?"

Back from another victorious encounter with the prince, we were discussing the situation over dinner.

"Kazuma, Kazuma. Wanna go out with me tomorrow? We could hit the casino. I'll call you 'Lord Kazuma' all day!"

"Pass. Didn't you use up all your money yesterday anyway? The heck were you doing all day today?"

Aqua had burned through the allowance Darkness had given her almost immediately after arriving in town. But now she proudly showed me a bulging purse. "I was at the Adventurers Guild today. You remember how Iris killed all those monsters on the way here? Being as smart as I am, I collected the valuable bits and pieces from them."

"So you sold the parts from the monsters she killed? Hand it over. I won't insist on all of it, but give us at least half. I'll make sure it goes to Iris."

I reached for the purse, but Aqua grabbed it instead, curling around it defensively.

"Um, Elder Brother. I'm not an adventurer, so I'm not eligible to sell monster parts. It's not that big a deal to me…"

"Sorry, Iris. If you give this lady an inch, she'll take a mile."

Aqua had apparently decided we were going to come after her, because she jumped up and got in a fighting stance. As she and I squared off, Megumin finished her meal, wiped her mouth, and said, "I will go along to babysit Aqua tomorrow. Otherwise, I'm sure she would run up a huge debt at the casino."

Hmm, well, at least Megumin didn't seem as likely as Aqua to develop a horrific gambling addiction.

"Me, I'm done investigating, so I'm not sure what I'm going to do tomorrow."

Aqua perked up at that, slithering over to Darkness. "Say, Darkness, in that case, why don't you come with us tomorrow? As a much more experienced casino-goer, I'll give you all sorts of tips."

"…You're not planning to beg me for more cash as soon as you run out of money, are you?"

It looked like that was exactly what she was planning. Nonetheless, I ignored Aqua's puffed-out, angry cheeks and said, "You guys do whatever. Let us handle the support funding. We'll squeeze every last eris out of that punk prince."

And so…

"Too bad! You lose again!"

"But hoooowwww?!"

It had been a week since Iris and I had started coming to the castle to "negotiate." Iris didn't have to fight anymore. They had run out of opponents. So that left me to battle for our budget.

The prince and I would have two bets each day. He just had to find the coin, nice and simple, and the very simplicity of it seemed to inflame his refusal to back down from the challenge.

"You did it, Elder Brother! Our defense budget is back to normal! Now we have to do something about what we originally came here for: the money for an offensive against the Demon King's army..."

"Wh-whoa, hold on! I can't give you money for that. Funding defense is one thing, but giving you money to attack the Demon King would cause all kinds of problems."

I'd assumed the prince would be game for another round of betting, but he was surprisingly adamant about this.

"Oh, so you're okay losing to me? You're okay with everybody knowing that the high-and-mighty ruler of the country of casinos got owned by some no-name outsider?"

But no matter how mercilessly I teased him, the prince only snorted. "You think you can get me with such obvious entrapment? The only reason I kept taking your bets was that the worst that could happen to me was that things would go on just like they always have—and if I won, I would have an official excuse to cut off your funding. But our nation doesn't want to antagonize the Demon King. There's no way I can give you money to attack him."

I was starting to think this prince was sharper than I had been giving him credit for. No choice. It was time to show my hand.

"You sure about that? You might win the next one, eh?"

"Nonsense. I've lost every single one of our bets so far; I have no reason to think I would start winning now. What do you take me for? I'm the prince of the Kingdom of...Casinos...?" His mouth fell open as if in slow motion. His eyes were locked on my right hand, which I held out, open, in front of him.

A few minutes ago, he had bet on my left hand and lost.

"Elder Brother, is it possible that the coin isn't in *either* of your hands and never has been?" Iris asked, surprised, though not as surprised as the prince.

"You got it. You're a smart girl, Iris. I'll bet you remember what I said when I made that first bet, right?"

"What you said? Um… I think it was '*The game couldn't be simpler. Guess where the hundred eris coin is,*' right? …Oh!"

"Argh!" The prince seemed to get it at the same time Iris did.

"Yep: I said '*where,*' not '*which hand.*' I was asking about the location of the coin. And I put it in my back pocket every single time!"

"Wow! You're so shrewd, Elder Brother! Nobody is as good at dirty tricks as you are!" Iris said, her eyes shining.

"That's a compliment, right?"

"Yes, I think so." Iris giggled, leaving me with the distinct impression that she wasn't complimenting me at all.

"You lowborn—filthy—son of a—! How dare you pull such a cheap prank on me! Don't you consider your actions a blemish on the name of royalty?!"

"Not at all."

Seeing as I wasn't a royal.

One hissing, furious breath escaped the prince when he saw my reaction. "…Grrr, this is why nobody likes country rats! Well, forget it. Shame on me for not seeing through your little ploy. I'm the one who's supposed to be the ruler of a country of casinos. I'll let you keep the money." He never did rise to our bait. "I won't be moved, no matter how much you mock me. The money for defense will continue as before but nothing more. That's absolutely the end of it… Though, to be fair, it was Lugkraft who said we needed to end your funding. Me, I just didn't want to get hitched to some girl from the sticks, so I went along with it. I regret that I never beat you, but hey, that was fun." He sounded so casual. "Right, see you later, then. I'll be praying you can beat the Demon King."

I was still trying to process something I had never thought he would say when the prince ushered us out of the room.

"—And that's the story. I have half a mind to smack that kid around a little bit."

"Good. Well said, Kazuma. To think, a country like Elroad, whose only redeeming feature is its ability to bring in money, making light of a nation like our Belzerg! And to have dragged Lady Iris through this— I'll kill that little brat myself!"

Back at the inn, I was having a secret meeting with Darkness and the others. Iris had gone to her room by herself, clearly depressed.

"I do not have any objection, of course. I would be happy to assault a castle or whatever you wish. My minion she may be, but she is still my comrade, and I shall not stand to see her made fun of. No Crimson Magic Clan member would remain calm in light of this."

"I don't know what you're planning, but I got those monster parts from Iris. I'll help out, as long as it's not anything scary, okay?"

I discovered I had two very eager friends and one sort of eager, maybe, I wasn't sure friend.

"I'll make that little sod regret underestimating me…!"

For quite a while now, I'd been nursing a plan we could use on the off chance we didn't get the defense money. Now it was time to fill everyone in…

4

Ah, morning. The sun poured in through the window, filling the dim room with gentle light. It was a beautiful day. A gorgeous way to wake up…but my mood had hit rock bottom.

"Let me out of here! What charge? I demand to know what charge you're holding me on! This is unwarranted detention!"

Aqua was shouting and banging on the bars despite the fact that it was the crack of dawn.

That's right: We were in jail. Unbelievably, my perfect, flawless plan hadn't worked. The local authorities had detained all of us and relieved us of our weapons and equipment.

The police building was made of stone, but considering the season, it was surprisingly warm. The jail itself was stone, too, with iron bars

on the cells. Inside each cell were only two things: chains for subduing violent prisoners and a really crappy toilet (pun intended).

Darkness was seriously bugging me: For some reason, she was just sitting there, not moving a muscle, staring at those chains and blushing faintly.

A jail guard who was outside filling out some paperwork frowned at Aqua's commotion. "Ch-charges…? I didn't think you'd be dumb enough to ask, but… You lot were sneaking around town in the middle of the night, then you used a huge magic spell that made a loud *boom*, and you thought no one was going to be upset?"

Megumin grabbed the bars of the cell. "In the city I live in, the police just let me off with a warning: *'We don't want the local terrain to change too much, so maybe you could pick a more distant spot.'* And this is the very first time I've let off magic anywhere near this town. You people are awfully intolerant."

"Idiot! That makes your police the weird ones!" (Well, he wasn't wrong.) "The townspeople here all jumped out of bed thinking a battle was starting! The prosecutor will be here soon. Save your excuses for her. Just waking people up with some magic isn't likely to get you in that much trouble. My guess is they'll let you off with a fine. Pipe down until then."

The night before, we had waited until everyone was asleep, then sneaked out of town, being careful to avoid the guards.

Initially, I'd asked everyone to make a little noise just outside town, thinking that all we needed was a bit of a commotion at the castle. But Megumin started going on about how if there was a medium-size hill nearby, she could make her Explosion reach all the way to the castle; it was okay; she was used to it… I didn't really know what she was talking about, but we went with that.

So we set off the blast, and in the ensuing chaos, I sneaked into the castle. I worked my way to the prince's bedroom, where I left a knife and a note by his pillow.

The note read: *Foolish human, did you think that a simple declaration of neutrality would save you? When we have brought low vile Belzerg, you will be next!*

…See? We make him think the Demon King's army wasn't interested in respecting any neutrals and scare him into joining our side. It was my specialty: cause a problem myself, then be the hero by solving it. This would put the fear of God, or at least of the Demon King, into him and might get him to cooperate…

That was the plan, but…

Come dawn, just as we could hear people waking up and starting their days, the woman appeared.

She was impeccably dressed, with a face that screamed competence, her red hair tied back in a ponytail and her piercing gaze fixed on us.

She reminded me of Sena, the prosecutor I'd met back in Axel. Sena had been as equally sharp-looking and scary. I wondered if she was doing well. A rumor I'd heard suggested she had solved a certain case and been welcomed back to the capital with open arms.

This prosecutor hung her jacket on the wall, poured herself some tea or something, glanced at us in the cell, and then turned a wordless look on the guard. *Who are these bums?* she seemed to ask.

"Late last night, we rushed to investigate the use of explosion magic outside of town, and we found this lot running around, pursued by a gathering swarm of undead. We didn't believe anyone would deliberately leave town to hunt undead at that hour, so we brought them in. The report is over there, ma'am." He pointed at a table and the paper on top of it.

Outside our cell, the jail was carpeted, and besides the table there was even a sofa and some chairs. I had to say, this didn't feel much like a place for holding or interrogating criminals.

The prosecutor must have read something in my look, because she took a sip of her tea and said, "You're in Elroad: a country that has prospered by running casinos. It's not a place that violent criminals usually visit. More typically, this building holds drunken tourists or people who've gambled away so much money, they can't even pay for an inn. It gives them somewhere to spend the night without freezing... Now, I'd like to speak to you each one by one." There was a cold flash in her eyes.

It looked like the interrogations were to be conducted right in front of the rest of us, maybe on purpose. We wouldn't be escorted to some cramped side room; she would ask her questions at the table in the carpeted area. The guard would stand behind the subject of her interrogation, watching for any false moves.

She apparently intended to speak to each of us individually, but I thought the whole point of interrogating suspects one by one was so they couldn't share their story with everyone else and you might be able to catch them in a contradiction.

The prosecutor had that covered, though. She pulled out a little item that was all too familiar to me.

"All right, I've got a few questions for you... Incidentally, this is a magic item that jingles whenever someone tells a lie. Thus, I'm afraid, any attempt to coordinate your stories is doomed to fail." She set the little bell on the table. Then she wove her fingers together, turning her stare on the person across from her.

"...Ahem, I may not look like much, but I am a Crusader. On the name of my patron goddess, Eris, I swear that I shall tell the truth and nothing but the truth."

...Yes, there was Darkness, beet red, her eyes weirdly eager.

The prosecutor let out a soft whisper of "Very good." With her eyes still fixed on the paper in front of her, she started talking. "Your class is Crusader. Your faith, the Eris sect... Please begin by stating your name."

"I refuse," Darkness said flatly.

"...Excuse me?" The prosecutor looked up in surprise, casting a dubious gaze at her.

"I said, I refuse. If you want to know my name, pry it out of me with interrogation or torture! But by the proud name of the Dustiness household, I shall never speak without a fight!"

"Miss Dustiness, is it? ...Don't worry—we have no intention of interrogation or torture or any such thing. Magic provides us far more

accurate access to truth than those outdated practices. You can relax…
But the Dustiness household? Do you mean *the* Dustiness household?
…I almost can't believe it… But the bell didn't ring…" She looked
questioningly at the magic bell, muttering to herself.

…Maybe it would be best if she just talked to me and let me do all
the explaining. I could see what was about to happen to this prosecutor,
and I felt downright sorry for her.

"Very well, Miss Dustiness. Could you tell me why you unleashed
magic in the place that you did?"

"I refuse. If you want me to talk, you'll have to wring every word
from my battered, broken body."

Darkness was still playing at resisting the questioning. What a lot
of trouble she was.

"…You understand your refusal to answer could be taken as an
admission of wrongdoing, yes? I told you already, we don't rely on outdated practices, but we aren't without some equipment here. I promise
you: I don't want to use it. You needn't worry; you're not going to be pun-
ished too harshly. So don't make this any harder than it has to be. Just tell
me what happened. I *am* authorized to use torture if, in my judgment, a
suspect is hiding something germane to the case at hand. I advise you not
to be rash about—"

"Yes, torture me! Do your worst! Please!" Darkness shouted, leaning
across the table. The prosecutor slid back a little. Then she looked at the bell.

…Of course it didn't ring.

Her frown deepened. "I… I believe I've heard enough from you…
Next suspect!"

"How could this happen…? I might never have another chance in my
life to be subjected to interrogation and torture. And it's over just like that…"

"You need to stop making people's lives harder because of your own
deviance."

A deeply disappointed Darkness had come back to the cell in
exchange for Megumin, who was next on the questioning list. The

prosecutor already looked so tired, it was almost painful to see. She collected herself when Megumin sat down, though, fixing her with a fittingly stern glare and putting her hands on the table. "...Now then, you're the one who actually let off the spell, correct? Your class is Arch-wizard, I assume. Please begin by stating your name."

"My name is Megumin."

The prosecutor didn't move and didn't soften her expression. "...I'm sorry, what did you say?"

"I said, Megumin."

The prosecutor waited for the bell to ring.

...Which, of course, it didn't.

At that, Megumin said, "Hey, if you have something to say about my name, then I shall hear it."

"N-no! I'm sorry—that was rude of me," the prosecutor said, startled. "Ahem. If I may ask, why did you use such a noisy spell in the middle of the night?"

"I make it my business to let off one explosion each and every day. Back in Axel Town, I sometimes used the spell in the middle of downtown as a fireworks display."

The prosecutor froze. But when she looked at the bell—still no ringing.

Megumin hadn't exactly answered her question, but the prosecutor seemed more interested in this idea of one explosion per day. "...So what happens to you if you don't perform this daily explosion?"

"I am loath even to think about it. I could all too easily picture myself simply going *pop*."

I wondered what it meant to go *pop*.

The prosecutor seemed to have the same question; she looked at the silent bell and muttered to herself. Why *didn't* that bell ring? Maybe Megumin really would go *pop*?

"Let's try a different question. The very act of using explosion magic in the middle of the night. What do you think about it? Do you not feel it's rather bad behavior?"

"I do not. The reason is that I was, in my previous life, none other than the goddess of destruction. Thus, I view destructive activity as right and good."

As Megumin babbled, the prosecutor glanced at the bell again. No ring.

…Maybe it was broken?

"Hey, Aqua, you're looking so great today, a guy could fall head over heels for you."

"Ooh, what's this all of a sudden? What's gotten into you, Kazuma? Maybe you really are feeling a little jealous about me getting chatted up by those guys the other—"

Diiing.

Before Aqua could finish, the bell on the table jingled.

"…Please don't interfere with the questioning."

"Sorry, I was just making sure the bell wasn't broken… Whoa! Hey, stop that! What are you doing?! How dare you try to strangle me after I complimented you! Besides, you did the same thing when you thought the bell was broken!"

I had to peel Aqua off me as she tried to wring my neck, but at least the prosecutor looked relieved to know that the bell was obviously in good working order.

"All right, I'll ask you again," she said. "Why did you set off an explosion in the middle of the night?" It almost sounded like she had softened toward Megumin a little bit.

"Because that is the way I live my life."

The prosecutor toughened right back up. She gave the bell a long, hard look, but…

"………Erm, next, please…," she said, drained, her shoulders slumping at the silent bell.

"My name? Aqua. I'm sort of the babysitter for these three—the overseer, you might even say."

The three of us looked at her, shocked. Then we looked at the lie-detecting bell on the table.

"Miss Aqua... Ahem. That's the same name as the goddess of water," the prosecutor said, but for some reason, the bell didn't ring.

...*Huh?*

"Hey, that thing's not ringing..."

"It doesn't ring so long as the speaker believes what she's saying," Darkness said. "Remember how it didn't ring even though Megumin was talking total nonsense?"

"Hey, I shall have you tell me just what total nonsense you are referring to."

If that was true, then did Aqua really think of herself as our guardian? I would have to knock the notion out of her later.

"All right, let's begin. Why in the world were you where you were at the time you were there?"

"We were keeping our friend, that perpetually horny guy Kazuma over there, clear of the town because we were afraid he might go sneaking into people's houses in the night."

Grrr! She must have thought she was getting payback on me for that stuff I said earlier to make the bell ring. I assumed that this, like the pronouncement about being our babysitter earlier, was just something she had convinced herself of in her broken mind, but...

The prosecutor and I both looked at the bell, but it didn't ring.

The prosecutor looked at me, contempt creeping into her gaze.

It... It's not true.

Seriously, did that bell even work?

"Erm, all right... And why did you use explosion magic in the middle of the night...?"

"To protect this city from an encroaching horde of monsters. You heard me: Those three and I saved the day, even though it was the middle of the night!"

Now Aqua was absolutely lying through her teeth, but still the bell didn't ring.

The prosecutor was wilting in the face of the silent bell. "... You're...not lying, it would seem. Incredible... You saved this city...?"

She looked directly at Aqua, suddenly abjectly apologetic. She sat up straighter. "Allow me to thank you on behalf of this city. Miss Aqua, wasn't it? And your class is Arch-priest?"

Suddenly, Aqua stood up from her chair. And then...!

"Heh-heh, Arch-priest is merely my disguise! I have nothing to hide: I am myself the very goddess of water! Yes! The goddess Aqua stands before you!"

We, the prosecutor, and even the guard all immediately looked at the bell.

...Which didn't ring.

Finally the prosecutor sighed and murmured, "Pfah. It's just broken..."

"Why doesn't anyone be*lieve* me?!"

A few minutes later, Aqua rejoined us in the cell after the guard had subdued her.

Having dealt with my three companions, the prosecutor told the guard to take the tinkling magical item to the back, then rubbed her eyes in exhaustion.

...I sort of felt bad for her. My pity for the prosecutor moved me to whisper to Aqua as she came back, "Hey, why didn't the bell ring for you? Did you use some clever spell?"

"That bell detects the ill spirit that emanates from a person when they tell a lie," Aqua said. "But I'm a goddess, remember? A little white lie here or there isn't enough to make evil emanate from me. And even if it did, my intense holy aura would wipe it out immediately. To make that bell jingle, I would have had to tell one hell of a whopper."

She sounded completely nonchalant. Sometimes she was capable of sort of...remembering she was a goddess and making use of her powers. I wasn't going to decide whether that was good or bad.

"...Huh? So it has to be a really big, really serious lie to make the bell ring? But back at our mansion, you made one of those bells go off when you praised me. That would mean..."

"All right, the last of you... Over here, please."

I was about to subject Aqua to an interrogation of my own when the cell door opened again and I was taken over to meet the poor prosecutor, her voice tremendously tired.

"I am so, so sorry! I had no idea I was dealing with someone related to both the Dustiness and Sinfonia households!"

The prosecutor had sure changed her tune in a hurry.

It was those pendants that Darkness and Claire had given me. The moment she saw them, the woman just about threw herself on the ground apologizing.

"Er, yeah, well, it's true that we set off an explosion in the middle of the night. But…y'know. We had a good reason for it. We just can't tell you what it is. Look, your country and ours are allies, right? Nobody's supposed to know we're here right now, so we'd like to keep this quiet…"

"Yes, of course. I understand! This could be a diplomatic incident if not handled delicately! You can spare me the details!"

Wow. Shows what noble privilege gets you. These items I'd obtained were so powerful, they could even silence a prosecutor.

"Okay, so can we go home now?" I asked.

The prosecutor smiled, practically relieved by the question. She made a point of seeing us to the door of the police station.

And then it happened.

"Ma'am, you said this bell was broken, but I'm afraid I can't find any evidence of malfunction. For the time being, I'll have it exchanged for good measure… Heeey, put this thing in the storage area; we'll get a new one!"

That was the guard from earlier, calling out to someone else.

At that, the prosecutor looked concerned. Probably trying to reconcile that with Aqua's claim that she was a goddess…

Then she glanced at me. "…If I may. The thing that blue-haired woman said earlier. Something about you running amok in the town at night on account of your overweening sexual desire…"

"That's a lie! All completely untrue!" I insisted, but the prosecutor took a step away from me all the same.

"I—I see. In any event, I won't say anything, so…"

Darkness patted my shoulder. "Look, uh… We believe you anyway. You aren't the kind of guy who would do anything to us, even if we were alone with you and completely defenseless. So that's great."

Diiing.

The room was filled with ringing when Darkness spoke.

The prosecutor took another step back.

"No one believes that Kazuma is the kind of man who would do such a thing. I certainly do not ever sleep with one eye open when it's his turn to tend the campfire."

Diiing.

…Wordlessly, the prosecutor took another step away from us.

Then our most obtuse party member clenched her fist and…!

No, this one I wasn't worried about. I knew it had to be a really big lie before the evil aura would do anything.

"Me, I trust you, too! You aren't the least bit horny, Kazuma, and you've definitely never tried to sneak into Darkness's bed, and I know that if anything, you're actually *too* kind and caring! Everything I said earlier was a complete and total lie!"

Ding, ding, ding, diiiiiing…

"*Ding* this, *ding* that, stop with the ringing already! Is that how you see me, you bunch of lousy—?! But I am *slightly* realistic about myself, so I'll change. Just stop saying that stuff; I'm sorry!"

5

Iris was waiting for us, tears in her eyes, when we got back to the inn.

"Elder Brother, thank goodness you're safe! When I heard you had all been arrested, I was afraid I would have to break you out even if I started a war in the process…"

"All right, calm down. I'm fine, everything's fine, nothing happened to us!"

It took a little while, but my militant martial princess finally got herself under control.

"But why in the world did you get arrested at all, Elder Brother? An employee here at the inn informed me that you had been taken in, but they didn't know any more than that…"

We had pursued our plan in secret, but Iris was too smart and too sharp not to figure it out sooner or later. When we explained what had happened, she looked at the floor, motionless. Darkness reached out a hand placatingly. "L-Lady Iris…? Um, I apologize for undertaking this action with Kazuma without consulting you. But I assure you, I thought it was for the best…"

"…ful…," Iris murmured instead of answering.

"Lady Iris?" Darkness asked again.

"…Shameful," Iris repeated, perfectly loud enough for us to hear this time.

At that, Darkness, with no trace of her usual stupidity and nonsense, bowed down in front of Iris. "I give you my most heartfelt apology, Lady Iris. Our indiscretion in this matter was entirely my own doing. I beg you to—"

But Iris silenced her with an upraised hand. "It was myself I was calling 'shameful.' I was hardly able to get anything from our negotiations and had to let my elder brother do most of the work… And then when I was unable to achieve my original mission of getting additional funds, I simply shut myself in my room, downhearted. Even though I had hardly even tried anything."

No, Iris, you tried really hard. If you hadn't been so strong, none of those contests would have taken place.

Despite my feelings, though, Iris shook her head. "While I was in here sulking, you and Lalatina put yourselves on the line, Elder Brother. That should have been my job."

Uh, no, actually, a princess shouldn't be doing stuff like that.

But I didn't think that blunt comeback was the best thing for Iris right now.

Then Iris picked up the sword leaning against the wall nearby and turned to Darkness, who was still kneeling. "Lalatina Ford Dustiness. I shall now attend the castle. Accompany me."

"L-Lady Iris?" Darkness looked up, surprised to suddenly be called by her full name. When she saw Iris's face, her cheeks flushed, and she gave a bow of her head befitting an actual knight.

"I am going to ask that Prince Levy provide us the additional funds. Indeed…" This was not the Iris I had first met. And it wasn't the one I'd come to know, with her easy laughter, quick anger, and curiosity about everything. "On the very name of Belzerg, by the blood I have inherited from the Hero of old. Whatsoever I need do, I shall have that money, even if I must force the matter!"

"Truly, you are a woman of resolve, Lady Iris! I, Lalatina, stand ready to defend you, come what may!"

The Iris I saw now was without question the descendant of an old hero. She stood with her blue eyes blazing, a warrior queen on the cusp of battle.

On the huge main street leading to the castle. Iris moved like a gale, a force of nature passersby instinctively gave a wide berth.

"Kazuma, get a load of Lady Iris today! Ahhh, to see my mistress walking so proud and so tall… As a noble charged with protecting my nation, I've never been happier!"

Darkness, sounding a lot like the Iris-obsessed, white-suited Claire, walked a half step behind the princess. Even she looked different than usual.

"Gotta admit, Iris is looking awfully cool, but your typical absurdity kind of offsets it. You're not much of a squire, but you're all she's got, so straighten up a little."

That struck a nerve; Darkness bit her lip, but at least she was self-aware enough to wipe the grin off her face.

I continued: "So, what, does Iris have some sort of plan? She said she would do whatever she had to and force the issue if necessary, so...? You guys gonna storm the treasury or something?"

"You impudent fool! I can't believe you think Lady Iris would ever stoop to such a thing! ...But if she plans to do whatever she has to, then I assume she's got some options in mind. I've heard of something Belzerg used to do back when it was first founded and had no money..."

Well, if there's such a great plan around, freakin' tell me about it already.

But it happened before I could get out the words.

"Is something the matter, Princess Iris? I'm afraid the prince has specifically ordered us that neither you nor any of your associates are to be admitted to the castle, so I beg your forgiveness, but—"

"Exterion!"

No sooner had we arrived than a guard tried to stop us—a guard Iris summarily ignored as she sliced open the great castle gate.

The huge, seemingly impenetrable door collapsed in a single blow, falling to the ground with a dull *thud*.

"Princess Iris?! Wh-what in the world...?!"

Iris continued to ignore the confounded soldier as she strode boldly through the now-open gate. The guard, realizing he wasn't up to handling this alone, grabbed a whistle hanging around his neck.

Fweeee!

The high-pitched sound echoed all over the castle grounds.

The path to the audience chamber was shin-deep with toppled knights and soldiers. Struck with the flat of Iris's blade, they grunted and groaned.

"Y-you kn-kn-know what this m-means, don't you?!" stammered the prince. He stood in front of Iris, desperately trying to keep his cool as he faced her unsheathed sword.

I whispered to Darkness beside me. "Hey, I know I said this before, but are you sure we're really necessary here?"

"H-hush! Be quiet! We've got him right where we want him!" she said, but the flush in her cheeks hinted that she got what I was saying.

Aqua, sticking close behind me, was put off by Iris's display of violence. "Hey, Kazuma, I'm starting to get worried about Emperor Zel. I want to go home and check on him. I'm sure he's crying his fuzzy little eyes out over how much he misses me."

"I'm pretty sure he forgets everything about three seconds after he learns it, so I wouldn't worry about him." I took a firm hold of Aqua's feather mantle to keep her from fleeing the scene.

Things seemed to be heating up with the prince in the meantime. "Now, you listen to me, you despicable curs! You know this amounts to a declaration of war! And I'm sure the other countries that support you won't stand idly by, either! This is going to be a major diplomatic—!"

"Prince Levy." Iris silenced the overexcited ruler with nothing but his name. Behind the boy, the prime minister was backing away uneasily. "I only wished to speak with you. I apologize for the more uncouth among my actions, but then, as you say, my people are but barbarians. Could I not urge you to overlook what I've done as the indiscretion of a simple rube?"

The prince nearly lost his head with rage. "Wha…?! That's the stupidest excuse I've ever…!"

"If such excuses will not prevail—"

Another voice now spoke quietly—not Iris but someone behind me.

Megumin took a big step forward, her eyes bright red, her staff upraised. "Then, my explosion magic and Iris's blade together shall bring this country to ruin…"

"Wh-wh-what did you say?!"

"Megumin, my friend, I must beg you not to be so hasty! I have no intention of doing any such thing!" Iris shoved Megumin back, out of the spotlight, but now her momentum was gone and she blushed a little.

"And what exactly do you intend to ask for? I assume you're after more money, but no amount of threatening will squeeze more cash out of me…!" Even cornered, the prince was still a royal; he didn't give a single inch.

"This is something my nation, Belzerg, used to do often, back when we were a new country and without money…" Iris drove her sword into the floor of the audience chamber. "Tell me: What is the largest, most dangerous, most destructive monster in this country?"

She was looking straight at the prince.

"I, Iris Stylish-Sword Belzerg, shall slay it, I vow."

Then she grinned.

1

A dragon.

It was the most major of monsters, a creature known to every single person not just here in this world but also back on Earth, where dragons didn't even exist. It was the biggest, baddest, most fearsome monster around. Anyone who killed one deserved to be called a hero and could demand any reward they wanted.

And we were hunting the king of dragons.

"Nooooooo! Noooooooooooooooooooooo! Noooooooooooooooooooo oooooooooooo!"

"Stop screeching and come with us! We're facing the mother of all badasses, and we're going to need all the help we can get—even you!"

That's right: We were going to slay a dragon.

Let's rewind to the moment when Iris awesomely said she would slay any monster.

"You'll exterminate the most destructive monster in our realm? The biggest and most awful? Don't make me laugh! I know you're strong, but that's biting off more than you can chew!"

The prince was practically spitting at us, but Iris just cocked her head. "If I can't do it, then it isn't any problem for you, is it? I'm simply going to defeat this monster of my own volition. If I should happen to lose my life in the process, you have my assurances that it won't reflect poorly on you. I'll be sure to leave behind a note elucidating all this."

"That's not my point! Nobody wants to see someone die, even if they've only talked with them a few times! I can't let you commit suicide!" The prince was red in the face now. He might have been an idiot, but apparently, deep down, he wasn't a completely terrible guy.

"Hmph, what has you so afraid? Indeed, it may be difficult for Iris alone to defeat such a powerful foe. But she has with her the greatest mage in all of Axel. Now, Iris, let us go kick the butt of whatever beast is afflicting this nation!"

"Grrr…! You can only talk like that because you don't know what you're dealing with! Listen up: We're talking about a monster that's ravaging this country, has built its nest in a gold mine of all places, and even now is terrorizing the countryside. It's—"

"Wait a moment, please," the prime minister said, interrupting the prince before he could finish his rebuttal to Megumin. "Lord Levy, perhaps we could indulge them in this matter? After all, they have proposed it themselves. And imagine the riches we could gain if that thing was driven out of the gold mine. We've kept ordinary adventurers and knights from doing battle with it on the assumption that they would only succeed in antagonizing it, but Lady Iris has the blood of the Hero of Belzerg in her veins. I don't think she will be so easily defeated."

He was kind of leering at us, but I had no idea why. The prince, making no effort to hide his annoyance, snapped, "Fine, do whatever you want!" Then he pointedly looked away.

"Kill a dragon? Are you stupid or something? Have you all gone insane?!"

"Pipe down! This is the only way. Anyway, we've beaten generals of the Demon King and evil goddesses. At this point, a dragon sort of seems like a step down."

A country dominated by the gambling industry apparently didn't see the need to put themselves in danger against a dragon just to get back one gold mine. But for us, that mine represented an important source of funds, not to mention a quest tailor-made for a party of adventurers.

"You keep a dragon for a pet, right? So don't chicken out now. What, planning to abandon Emperor Zel when he grows up?"

"Please don't compare my dear, sweet Emperor Zel to any old dragon. He's very smart, so he would never attack a person. Compared to him, what's a feral dragon but a stupid lizard?"

I felt bad for the dragon, being called "stupid" by Aqua. Weren't dragons supposed to be highly intelligent?

"Lady Aqua, I shall be protecting everyone, so I beg you to work with me. I have to think that facing a dragon will prove difficult without support magic..."

Iris looked downright pitiful, and Aqua evidently couldn't keep complaining in the face of an imploring child. "...Bah, fine. I'll help you, so when you grow up and become a queen, you can pay me back by making the Axis Church the official state religion."

"That has *chaos* written all over it! You should count yourself lucky that the Axis Church hasn't been wiped out already!"

As Aqua and I argued, Iris suddenly snickered. When she realized we were both looking at her, she waved a hand quickly and said, "Oh, don't get me wrong! I've just, er, always been so taken with adventuring; I'm enjoying the feeling that I'm almost part of an adventuring party myself..." She looked down bashfully, and I remembered that back when we had swapped bodies, she'd seemed excited about adventuring.

Megumin, though, chuckled and said, "Now, this is not playtime, you understand? There is no end to the naïveté of these sheltered girls... But very well. I shall deign to teach my minion the fundamentals of adventuring."

"Thank you. I would like that very much!"

Darkness couldn't help smiling at the two of them—they acted like old friends—as Megumin began her lecture.

"...Ahem, Iris, look at this. You see how this branch is broken?

There is a very good likelihood it indicates the presence of a monster ahead."

"I don't think so. My Sense Foe skill would be going off."

Megumin shot me a look. Then she collected herself and started walking toward the mine…

"Iris, do you know what the most important thing to have on a lengthy adventure like this is? That's right: water. You absolutely must avoid being unable to rehydrate after a difficult challenge. So be sure to conserve your water supply as much as you—"

"Leave the water to us! Kazuma and I both know Create Water, so drink as much as you like; there will always be more!"

Megumin had been trying to give some advice to Iris, who was having a drink, but Aqua promptly produced more water with her spell. She filled up Iris's canteen, then walked away, satisfied. Megumin watched her, looking eager to snap something at her.

In due course, we came to a giant tree. "Iris, look! Look at the marks scratched into this trunk! I recognize this pattern. There's a hive of killer bees nearby; try to move as quietly as possible…"

"Okay, everyone take hold of me. I'll use my Ambush skill while we move up. That way the monsters won't see us."

"……" Megumin's mouth worked open and shut, and her eyes suggested she felt some conflicting emotions about me. But in the end, she grabbed hold like everyone else.

We went on that way for several hours.

"Now then, there are no major enemies in sight, so let us take a brief break. Iris, let me tell you the most important things to know when taking a break in the field. First, when you are in the territory of powerful monsters, you must never light a fire, because of the risk of attracting—"

"Ooh, Kazuma, Kazuma, use Kindle for me. I want some nice hot tea."

"You brought your tea set all the way out here? You're hopeless. Give me some, too. Here. *Kindle*." I used my magic to set fire to a pile of leaves and branches Aqua had collected.

"Grrraaahhhh!"

"Waaaah! Megumin, what are you doing? My poor fire went out!"

Megumin, who had suddenly attacked the fire with her staff, said, "Don't you ask me about what I am doing! Starting a fire here is sure to attract monsters—I've been trying to mentor Iris all day, and you two…!"

Just as she was shouting, I felt it. "My Sense Foe ability acted up a second ago. Careful, something's coming!"

There was a nasty cracking sound. We could see a flock of birds take to the sky, a sign that something very unpleasant was coming our way.

Aqua, still sore about her fire, exclaimed, "This is your fault for shouting, Megumin!"

"My fault?! Yes, I see, this is all my doing—I'm so sorry! I will apologize, but I do not have to like it!"

We hadn't even gone into the mine yet. I didn't know if this was good luck or bad.

The ground-rattling titan that came crashing through the woods made me understand why they called this creature the king of dragons.

I stopped trying to play it cool and just shouted:

"It's heeeerrrrre!"

A Golden Dragon drew near.

2

Dragons.

Hoarders of treasure and lovers of shiny things. Monsters whose defeat assured the slayer's fame and fortune.

And one of them had taken up residence in a gold mine, presumably drawn by the presence of, well, gold. Dragons were renowned for eating unusual things; maybe nibbling on the local minerals had given it this coloration.

"We've hit the jackpot, Kazuma! This is a Golden Dragon, the most valuable of all dragon species! If you eat its meat, your level shoots up, and its blood is an ingredient in that rare elixir: the skill-up potion. Its fearsome horns and scales can be turned into valuable weapons and equipment! This thing is a walking loot chest!"

Everyone was pretty freaked out by the sudden appearance of the dragon—everyone but Darkness, who hefted her great sword. "Lady Iris! I'll distract the dragon; you use the opening to attack from a safe position! I'm not much for offense myself…!" At the same moment, she activated her Decoy skill. She looked so cool doing it that I wondered where the muscle-brain we were all accustomed to had gone.

I wish she was always like this.

"All right, Megumin, start chanting Explosion! I don't want to vaporize a valuable monster if we can avoid it, but if Iris gets in too deep, then don't hesitate! Aqua, buff Iris and Darkness with support spells! I'll give you guys cover fire from a distance!"

"V-v-v-very well…! Ind-d-deed, even such a beast as a d-d-d-dragon is no more than a common lizard before my…my explosion…!"

"Hey, you negligent NEET! Don't hide behind us, shooting arrows—get up there and make yourself useful!"

The Golden Dragon, focusing its bloodshot eyes on Darkness, ran for the Crusader with a speed belying its size. Megumin, with no special talent for triumphing over adversity, trembled violently, while Aqua, despite her complaining, started casting defensive buffs.

I wanted to do something helpful, I really did, but there was only so much I could offer against a dragon. My attacks would never punch through its scales; there was a good chance I would die if I so much as got close to it.

"Have at me, Golden Dragon! Learn the power of House Dustiness, we who are known as the Shield Bearers!" Darkness, thoroughly buffed, didn't give an inch to the oncoming dragon but stood there with her armor gleaming in the sun. It looked like something out of a fairy tale. Meanwhile, I noticed that Iris, who had received attack buffs from Aqua, was startlingly still.

I glanced over at her to see that she had her sacred sword in hand; her eyes were closed and she wasn't moving a muscle. I could see something crackling through the air around her, almost like electricity, and my wealth of anime and manga knowledge told me instantly what was happening.

This was gonna be big.

Iris was getting ready to use her biggest, baddest move.

I knew how this went: You focused your entire spirit and your entire being into one devastating final attack that you used against your biggest enemy at your most desperate moment.

"*Karrrrooo, krrrrrooo…!*" The dragon, wary, wasn't making a move on Darkness. Dragons might be smart, but right now, that was the wrong choice.

Iris finally opened her eyes. The magic that had been filling the air around her was focused into her sword, which shone far brighter than usual.

But I noticed what was going on only after the dragon had spotted Iris and looked downright frightened.

"*Sacred Explode*!!"

Iris's yell contained her entire spirit. The hillside was enveloped in a blinding light—!

Elroad was practically bubbling with the news.

"The dragon is dead! The princess of Belzerg slew it!"

When we got back to town, we popped in at the Adventurers Guild to let them know we had taken care of the dragon.

Dragons are basically big lumps of magical energy. Every inch of them, not just their horns, scales, and fangs but every little drop of their

blood, is a valuable material. We let the Guild know about our successful expedition so they could go out and collect the pieces, and this commotion was what resulted.

A dead dragon had to be worth a pretty penny. But we weren't after the sort of sums they would pay out to individuals. We put the cheering "They're heroes! They're dragonslayers!" town behind us and headed for the castle.

"We've already heard the news! Incredible! To think the Golden Dragon could be defeated…!" The guard who had looked so skeptically at Iris before now bowed enthusiastically and respectfully the moment he saw us. Talk about flip-flopping… But the recognition did feel pretty good. "I don't suppose there's any chance you could share with me a few words about what sort of battle it was…?"

He was so cringey, so apologetic, I couldn't resist a grin. "It was a one-hit kill."

Granted, it was Iris who had landed the hit.

"One-hit?! O-one hit…?!"

We left the guard standing there with his mouth agape and walked straight for the audience chamber.

The Golden Dragon had been cut clean in half by Iris's attack. When the light had faded, I saw that the dragon was dead, and I had no idea what she could have done to it. But then…

"Iris, do not think this means you have triumphed against me! My Explosion could have defeated that dragon just as easily! It is only because we didn't want to reduce the dragon to dust that I deliberately, *de-lib-er-ate-ly*, held myself back!"

Megumin, who had not only been denied a golden opportunity but had been confronted with evidence of Iris's immense power, was beside herself.

"Yes, of course, Megumin, my friend. I understand, so please forgive me."

"I don't believe I shall! What is this Sacred Explosion of yours, and how dare you give it a name that suggests it surpasses even Explosion? I shall not allow you to use it again!"

"Um, the name is actually Sacred Explode, and I've heard it doesn't have anything to do with Explosion…"

"How can you say it has nothing to do with explosion magic when the name sounds like a cheap rip-off? Personally, I believe its immense destructive power is born from having such a similar name!"

"Miss Megumin, I have had just about enough of you! Please don't refer to my family's cherished hereditary technique as a 'cheap rip-off'! The name of the move has its roots in the name of this sword…!"

The two of them were still arguing as we entered the audience chamber where the prince was waiting, looking different from all the other times we'd seen him…

"Did you really do it?!" The prince was practically spitting, red in the face, when he heard the story of our battle.

"Yes, Your Majesty. Here is the Golden Dragon's horn for proof." Iris showed him the dragon horn she'd been carrying with her, causing chatter among the assembled audience. This room hadn't been very friendly at first; they'd seen us as nothing but a bunch of bumpkins. Maybe the dragon had been a real problem for them, or maybe being a dragonslayer simply made you that famous, but all of them turned warm, affectionate looks on Iris now.

How about that? Pretty darn good, huh? That girl is my little sister.

"A shining golden horn," the prince mumbled, almost to himself. "There's no question; this belonged to the dragon who lived in the gold mine…" The chattering picked up its pace.

That was when it happened.

"I ask you to wait." The growing excitement in the room was suddenly dampened by the voice of the prime minister, who regarded us with a cold stare. Ugh, he wasn't planning to make things even harder, was he? "I would expect no less from a princess with the blood of the

Hero in her veins. From a member of the clan that has inspired fear in the Demon King for generations… You there!"

He signaled to a soldier, who was holding a big leather pouch.

…I'm pretty sure that's not the extra money they promised.

We'd beaten enough generals of the Demon King that I had gotten a pretty good feel for how much money was inside a leather pouch of any given size. I could see this pouch contained the bounty for a major mark but not an entire payment of international support.

"…What's this?" Iris seemed to share my doubts, because she looked distinctly confused as she took the bag.

"It's your reward for the defeat of the dragon on this occasion. It includes a little extra on top of what we would normally pay an adventuring party to handle the quest. Take it and go."

"But—!"

The prime minister's words caused something of an uproar. This was supposed to be an away game, but a lot of the muttering sounded sympathetic to us.

But there was another surprise in store.

"W-wait, Lugkraft! I don't think I can countenance this… L-look, I understand. I know all the trouble we'd invite by giving them further monetary support. But even so, to give dragonslaying heroes such a paltry sum…"

I had been under the impression that the prince didn't think much of Iris. But he was the one suddenly arguing on our behalf. For a little while now, he had been looking at Iris very much the way one would look at a hero. He may have been a prince, but I guess he was also still a boy. He idolized dragonslayers.

But.

"My prince, I've already explained to you numerous times. We should have cut off even payments in support of their defense, but failing that, it is certainly not in our nation's interest to support an offensive on their part… Lady Iris, I do recognize your situation. But you must know that we have pressing circumstances of our own to deal with. I beg you to understand."

The prince looked downcast.

…Pressing circumstances? I'd been so sure they were just being mean to Iris. What was he talking about?

Unhappily, the prince raised his eyes to look at us—no, at Iris. "Ahem… I'm sorry. There are reasons we can't give you any more funds. You heard the prime minister. Please forgive us."

Then he gave a deep and contrite bow of his head, his self-important attitude gone without a trace. Even I couldn't say much to that, let alone Iris or Darkness.

"Gosh…" Naturally, though, Iris was awfully upset. She unconsciously grabbed my arm with shock, standing vacant and motionless.

The prince was understandably bothered by the sight. "Listen, er… That's it—have you been to the casino yet? You're all too serious for that sort of thing. I'll bet you haven't been to our country's famous casinos, have you? You should check them out, cheer yourselves up!"

That didn't sound very encouraging…

………

"Er, Your Majesty. If I may?"

"Hrm? What is it? Your little sister and I have no further—"

"No," I said, knowing that I was speaking out of turn. "It's about the casinos. I'd like to go big before I go home. Is there any way we could, you know, get a free pass to the biggest, bettingest casino around?"

"…Your little sister is in the dumps, and that's how you act? Are you insane? No, no, I was the one who suggested a change of scenery at the casino, so I suppose you can do what you want. A word of warning. Cheap tricks like the one you played on me won't work there, all right? Our casinos aren't so easily hoodwinked. They built this country. So I won't try to stop you, but—"

Before he could finish, I had to bow my head with exaggerated politeness—to hide the grin on my face.

*   *   *

We were on the way home from the castle.

"…I was useless. I felt like I did my best, but it was all for nothing… And after all the help you and everyone gave me, Elder Brother. After the promise I made to everyone at home…"

Iris was walking at the tail of our party, sunk in a deep depression.

Darkness, maybe hoping to cheer her up, was about to call out when— "Kazuma, Kazuma. Isn't there something a big brother can do at a time like this? I cannot stand to see my minion in such low spirits."

Who exactly did she think I was? I wished there was some way *I* could immediately turn to me every time there was any kind of problem.

Aqua, who clearly hadn't followed everything that had happened, was walking at the head of the group, humming a short tune. I turned to my little sister, plodding behind us. "Yo, Iris." She flinched and drew into herself at that. She clenched her fists and dropped her head, probably worried that I was about to yell at her because things had gone so poorly. But I said, "I think you killed it in there. I mean, you're a dragonslayer now. That makes you a certified hero, and you can't do much better than that. I won't let anybody make a stink when you've got that sort of record."

Darkness gave a vigorous nod of agreement. "He's absolutely right, Lady Iris! You did your very best! When we get back home, I, Lalatina, shall tell everyone how bravely you fought the—!"

"So, Iris." I cut off Darkness, plopping a hand on my little sister's head.

"You just leave the rest to your big brother."

Then I smiled at her…

"Hey, Megumin, that's the Pat-and-Smile. He's trying to use the legendary skill that causes girls to fall in love with you instantly."

Okay, so I wasn't *not* hoping for that. But I wished Aqua could read the room.

3

"Just leave the rest to your big brother."

That's what I'd said to Iris, and I went on.

"I have an idea," I'd said.

"Why, you, you… You looked so cool, you got my hopes up—and now *this*?!"

The answer was blindingly simple: the casino.

With my naturally high Luck, gambling was the perfect way to make money.

Darkness wasn't especially happy to learn that we were pinning everything on something you could hardly even call a plan, but she didn't have any better ideas, so she had to go along with it.

"Say what you like, Darkness. I think this has an excellent chance of working."

"You're nuts! Going to the casino when you need to *make* money is the definition of a bad idea! I'm so sorry, Lady Iris; more fool me for having trusted this man…"

Iris, though, shook her head at the frankly very rude Darkness. "No, Lalatina. I agree that this is a good idea."

"Y-you do, Lady Iris?!" Darkness was completely thrown by this unexpected answer. "I have to beg you to reconsider. We have the money from the dragon that you risked your life to get, along with the support you won from the prince. I grant it isn't as much as we need, but compared to the impossible situation we were in when we first got here…!"

Darkness was trying to get her to think rationally by emphasizing the success Iris had already had. The princess, however, took Darkness's hand gently and said, "Lalatina. Lady Aqua, Arch-priest of the Axis Church, once told me: *'If all seems lost, just give it a shot. If you screw up, you can always run away.'*"

"That is poor advice, Lady Iris! Don't let yourself be contaminated by the Axis Church!"

I took Darkness's shoulder. "Don't grow up to be hardheaded like this lady, Iris. Come on—here's the casino. Casinos are fun."

"What do you mean 'hardheaded,' you lout?!"

I ignored the still-enraged Darkness, took the bag of support money from Iris, and traded it for a boatload of chips from a clearly startled clerk.

The first thing to do would be to shut Darkness up. It was going to be all right. I was a close personal friend of the actual goddess of Luck, after all.

I sat down at the roulette table and hefted about a third of my massive supply of chips into my hands. Everyone who saw me, including Darkness, goggled; only Iris watched with an expression of absolute seriousness. Hoping to reassure her and picturing my surprisingly combative Chief, who might be looking down on me at that very moment, I said, "Iris, let me reiterate: Contests are meant to be enjoyed. There's a special phrase you're supposed to say at times like this. I learned it from a friend with even better Luck than mine."

I put all my chips on red. Then, loudly enough that that surprisingly mischievous goddess in heaven could hear me—I needed only a little bit of help—I exclaimed:

"Let's give it a shot!"

A massive crowd had gathered around me; every customer in the casino seemed to be watching the roulette table.

"Ahhh-ha-ha-ha-ha-ha, a win! Another win! Good Lord, Kazuma, you have the best Luck I've ever seen! I would follow you my entire life, as long as we never left the casino!"

"Hey, quit acting all satisfied over my victory. What if you jinx me?"

I'd gotten a windfall.

The roulette dealer was almost in tears, but I had no reason to stop now.

"Hey, get me another coffee," I said to Darkness, who had completely calmed down and now listened to everything I said.

"S-sure thing—right away!"

I had been having her focus on bringing me caffeine to keep me awake and alert. When I'd won my first bet, she'd let out a sigh of relief. When I'd gotten the second one, I could see her exhale and smile grimly.

"Got it! I mean—here it is, sir! Here's your coffee!"

"Excellent."

The third time, she'd let out an audible "Wow." And by the fourth and fifth times, she had been practically immobilized with amazement.

"Er, excuse me, sir..." When I raked in my seventh and eighth piles of chips, the dealer looked at me with distinct respect.

"Hmm? What's up? If you tell me I can't bet anymore, I won't listen. You would never tell a customer who was losing big that you couldn't accept any more bets from him, would you?" I pulled out a bucket of clattering chips and placed it on the table. "I think it's time to start getting into some bigger bets. If I'm not mistaken, odds double if you bet on both the color and the number, right?"

"Sir! P-please, any more bets and...!" A guy who had been watching us from the crowd for a while now came over to me. I assumed he was the manager, because he was white as a sheet. If this had been a private establishment, I might have taken pity on them, but unfortunately for them, this casino was state-owned. I could take them for all they were worth and the only real victims would be that prince and his prime minister—i.e., no one I cared about.

I made a show of sipping the coffee Darkness had brought me, then pulled out the two pendants around my neck. "Hey, you know what these are?"

"...? ...Wh-what?! Crests of both the Dustiness and Sinfonia households, the most powerful families in Belzerg?!"

The manager, who clearly *did* know what these were, went even paler.

"You got it: I have two major noble houses standing behind me. Hear what I'm saying? If you tell me I can't bet anymore, then I'm *willing to bet* there's going to be a diplomatic incident."

"Hrk…!" The manager ground his teeth but backed away, glaring at me.

Heh, I win…again.

Iris had been watching excitedly; now she took my hands. "Amazing, Elder Brother! I heard you had good Luck, but I never imagined it was this good! With this kind of fortune, maybe you should have skipped adventuring and made your living at the casino."

Live the gambling life, huh? The thought had occurred to me, but if a trouble-magnet weak-ass Adventurer like me started winning big at the casino, I was sure someone would come after my life. Anyway, this sort of thing only works when you do it occasionally. When you get greedy and try to keep the gravy train rolling, that's when the trouble starts. The whole reason I could even do what I was doing at that moment was because I had the backing of a princess and two noble families, plus the pretext that I was trying to raise money to fight the Demon King.

Otherwise, I was pretty sure Lady Eris would have taken me to task for this little show.

"Nah, games of chance aren't my calling. You know me: I live to adventure in order to defeat the Demon King." I made sure I sounded as cool as possible; Iris turned eyes sparkling with respect on me.

I put the bucket full of chips on Black 6, sending a murmur through the crowd of onlookers.

"Now spin that wheel!"

Sweating but unable to say no, the dealer picked up a ball…!

"I'll take that same space!"

"Huh?!"

Before I could stop her, Aqua had put her chips on Black 6, too. At the same instant, the ball went plummeting onto the wheel, where it spun crazily.

"You—! I told you not to get cocky; this isn't a game!"

"Why can't I bet, you stingy NEET? I've been losing every round! I need to make something back…"

As I was busy yelling at Aqua, the ball slowly came to a rest…

"Red Five."

"Loooook at thaaaat!"

"Waaaah! I lost all my allowance!"

I motioned to Darkness to drag Aqua away.

"Hey, Darkness, please! I have to make some cash here or I won't be able to buy Emperor Zel a souvenir! Lend me some money, please? I'll pay you back when I win!"

"I'll buy you a dumb souvenir—just get over here! Our nation's future is at stake!"

I composed myself as I watched Aqua being dragged off. Now that the goddess of bad luck wasn't sitting next to me anymore, I should be able to get my groove back.

"Kazuma, Kazuma, the way to get back what you lost is to make a biiiig bet! All the chips you have left!"

"No way! Unlike you, I'm trying to be serious about this! Hey, don't grab my chips! Darkness, get her out of here, too!"

While Darkness handled Megumin just like she had Aqua, I put down a bet on Black 8.

"It's on!"

That night.

"Ooh, Kazuma, Kazuma. You were *so* cool today. Hey, you know what? There's something I've always wanted to tell you…"

"Heap all the praise on me you want; I'm not going to give you any money. Besides, you'd just copy my bets… Oh look, right on schedule."

We were heading back to the inn after a day of winning really, really big when something totally predictable happened.

"Hey, you there. Got a moment?" Several masked men blocked our path.

When Iris saw them, she looked up at me with genuine respect. "Elder Brother, that's incredible! You even foresaw this!"

"Right? I told you, they'll one hundred percent try to ambush us. These guys are hired muscle from the casino."

The men shook their heads almost frantically. "N-no we ain't! We're bandits who heard you came into a lot of cash! Leave the money with us and no one gets hurt. C'mon—we'll spare your l—"

I ignored the man and took out some Bind wire. "All right, guys, let's tie up these suckers and get one of those magic bells that jingles when you tell a lie! If the country or the casino is behind this, we'll make a big stink about it and squeeze even more money out of Elroad!"

That caused not only the men in front of us but, for some reason, my companions, too, to stare at me wide-eyed.

"K-Kazuma, you... So this is why you wanted to take dark back roads to the inn. And why you had Aqua buff you and why you insisted on full armor and equipment even though we were just going to the casino...," Darkness murmured. The men took a collective step back and held a whispered conference:

"This could be trouble. I feel like we're the ones who got trapped here."

"And ain't that a Crimson Magic wizard over there? Plus two girls with blond hair and blue eyes. And you know what that means..."

"Shit, there are nobles here?! A lotta nobles are nothing to sneeze at!"

Well, this wouldn't do.

"They're thinking about running away," I announced. "Don't let 'em! They're worth a fortune! Don't hold back! If worse comes to worst, we've got Aqua's Resurrection!"

Then I turned toward the men...!

"Run for it! This guy is trouble; he said he's got Resurrection or something! He's gonna eat us alive!"

"Don't let 'em catch you; run like the wind!"

"Wait! Wait for me!"

I guess I was right about these guys, because they ran for the hills.

"…You know, Kazuma, I'm not sure I like you bringing Resurrection into all this."

"Aw, I didn't really mean it! I was only trying to scare them! Seriously, I don't have the nerve to… Geez, why are you looking at me like that? It's true!"

Suddenly *I* was the villain, and I had to walk things back in a hurry.

4

After that, I started going to the casino on a daily basis.

"He's heeere!"

The blood would drain from the manager's face as soon as he saw me.

At first, I think they assumed I couldn't keep winning like I had been. Whenever I would show up, the manager would just watch from afar, storm clouds on his face. But as the days went by and the winnings I took home got bigger and bigger, he started to realize this was no laughing matter.

"Honored customer? You're so strong, and I'm afraid if we allow you into our establishment any more, we'll go broke. We're prepared to offer you a small honorarium, but I must ask—"

"This is a state-run casino, isn't it? You can't go broke. In the black, in the red—it doesn't matter. Plus, the prince himself told me to cheer myself up at the casino. Get a load of this: It's a special VIP card he gave me."

"Th-the prince?! I—I can hardly believe…"

I ignored the flabbergasted manager and went back to making my customary outrageous bets.

*   *   *

Several days after that. My bags of betting money had come to look sort of like a snowman, and I was starting to think I had about enough in there to make up the additional support funds.

"H-h-h-honored customer. Let me be quite honest with you. We are considering closing the casino for a while, starting tomorrow. Seeing as you seem to be, er, one of our most regular regulars, sir, I thought we should let you know…"

"Aw, is that right? Well, I came here ready to stay a few years to make all the money I needed, so I don't mind waiting. But if the casino's closed for too long, isn't that going to impact the country's bottom line?"

"A few *y-years*?"

I had them so desperate, they were ready to close the place to get rid of me.

"Sir, I beg you! Please! Please, no more! My superiors take me to task every single day! Please forgive me!"

"Aw, don't worry about it. I've got the prince's blessing, after all. You got a problem, take it up with him."

At long last, we had simply reduced the manager to tears.

We were on our way to the casino that morning for another day of gambling when we were met by a messenger from the castle.

The messenger brought us to the castle, where we were admitted directly to the audience chamber.

"I must humbly beg you to go back home."

Those were the first words out of the prince's mouth when he saw us, his head bowed low. It hadn't been that long since we saw him last, yet he looked haggard, beat down. Maybe it was my imagination.

"Hey, hey, you were the one who told Iris to go cheer herself up at the casino. And that's exactly what we're doing. When we feel cheerful again, we'll get out of here."

"Stop, we can't afford to have you pick us clean like this! Any more and it will be considered the same as if we had given you the support money!"

Well, yeah.

"So you call yourself the country of casinos, but when somebody wins big, you send them home? That sounds pretty sketchy to me. We're just enjoying ourselves at your establishment. You got a problem with that?"

"Hrrgh… Listen. Elroad has circumstances of its own…"

Yeah, you keep alluding to them. But that didn't have anything to do with us.

"These circumstances, what are they exactly? Could you possibly tell us about them?" Iris asked, stepping forward.

The prince looked unsure for an instant but then said apologetically, "No, I'm afraid they—"

He didn't make it to the end of his sentence.

"This nation of ours is engaged in negotiations with the Demon King."

The prime minister looked at us with total calm, despite the staggering thing he'd just said. The crowd didn't so much as stir, indicating that everyone in the room already knew about this.

"Lugkraft, you…!"

The prime minister kept speaking, cutting off the nervous prince. "Our nation is conducting peace talks with the Demon King's army. They would prevent his forces from moving against Elroad even if they should triumph over Belzerg. Our side of the bargain is that we will no longer provide you aid in your struggle against the Demon King."

He sounded so…nonchalant. Darkness bared her teeth at him. "You monster, you can't trust anything the Demon King says! As a member of the human race, you should be ashamed of yourself!"

"But it remains a fact that Belzerg has reached an impasse with the

Demon King's army," the prime minister said to the obviously enraged Crusader. "You're at a stalemate, and there's no way to know which of you will prevail. In such circumstances, when one receives an offer of non-harm in exchange for neutrality, it would be foolish to dismiss it out of hand." He frowned so that he at least seemed apologetic.

It wasn't like I couldn't sympathize; I didn't want to have anything to do with the Demon King, either. I was puzzling over how to wrap this up neatly when Darkness exclaimed, "You trust the Demon King…?! Let me tell you something about him: The Demon King will abduct a woman the moment he sees her—any woman, even a child—and make her his plaything. He's a despicable creature who kidnaps princesses and female knights, all to subject them to the most hideous depredations. That's the truth about your 'king'!"

"S-such impudence! Wait, where did you even get a story like that? Truth be told, my experience at the negotiations was that the great king was a very amiable fellow, a demon of the most trustworthy type…"

I thought the idea of a trustworthy demon sounded pretty questionable in its own right, but anyway, the prime minister was obviously keen on the Demon King. But…

"Where did I get it? I think that story is one of the more well-known ones… Some people also say that he's into little girls, some say that he's the biggest pervert on the entire continent and loves freaky role-play, and some even say that he's gay. I mean, I've heard all kinds of stories…"

"Who has been spreading these ridiculous rumors?!"

For some reason, all this really seemed to tick off the prime minister, but Aqua, standing there with a big grin on her face, announced, "That was the Axis Church! My children have been telling the stories I made up about him."

"Say, are you sure it isn't *your* fault the Demon King is so bent on attacking us?" I said.

The prime minister held his head and shook when he discovered that this was the doing of the Axis Church. A strike against someone you had chosen to trust was essentially a strike against you, so I could understand why he might want to make excuses for his negotiating partner. But still…

At that moment, Iris said, "Um, Prince Levy? I think I'm starting to see the situation here. You've been told that when Belzerg is defeated, Elroad will be next, and if you want to avoid that fate, you must work with the Demon King. Isn't that right? If, as the prince of this nation, you've considered the matter and feel this is the best way to survive, then I won't press you on it any further." As ever, she sounded sweet and self-less, eager not to say anything that might hurt her listener. "So I beg you to put your mind at ease. I'll speak to my father to ensure this will not harm relations between our countries going forward… I think of myself as, if nothing else, a fine judge of character—did you know that? I've known from the moment we first met that you don't actually hate me, my prince. I don't say that to sound pretentious. It is just a feeling."

The prince looked at the ground when he heard that.

"The royal family of Belzerg is very strong," Iris said. "So much so that we would not be defeated by the Demon King's army even without sup-port. So…" Her voice was gentle, like she was comforting a wounded child. "Please don't look so pained." Then she gave an absolutely innocent smile.

"…I'm given to understand that in the wider world, I'm known as the idiot prince," the young man admitted, sitting down on his throne. He looked at everyone around the room; I don't think any of us was expecting this change of topic. "They say I wash my hands of politics to spend all my time gambling." Finally, he turned to Iris, who was stand-ing with her mouth open, and gave her a grin that, for once, made him look like a boy his age. "How about you make one more bet with me? No tricks this time. And if you win just one more time… I'll place *my* bet on Belzerg defeating the Demon King!"

"M-my prince?!" the prime minister said in an agonized voice. But the prince was already pulling out a coin, hiding it behind his back. Then he thrust out his closed fists at me.

"So which hand is it in?"

5

That night—it was that awkward time when it was too early to go to sleep but too late to start anything else.

I assume I don't have to spell out how my little contest with the prince ended.

The prime minister threw a fit, but His Majesty's entourage looked surprisingly happy about the outcome. For all the rumors and talk, they seemed pleased that the person they served had finally made a decision of his own.

I had a feeling the "idiot prince" talk might die down after this.

So, in the end, defense payments for the fight against the Demon King would continue as they always had. We were also promised a large sum of money in the near future to help with an offensive. And on top of all that, Iris was bestowed with the nickname "Dragonslayer." So it was a pretty great result all around.

…There was just one thing still bothering me: The prince seemed a little too interested in Iris. He had been putting on the whole mean-guy act since our first meeting merely to drive a wedge between our two countries, but after everything was resolved, we had another big feast, and this time, he seemed pretty darn friendly.

That's right: There was an out-and-out reconciliation between the two of them.

I thought back to my original plan. After all, the whole reason I'd come along in the first place was to keep Iris from being given away to some know-nothing from nowhere. I'd been relieved to discover on our arrival that the prince himself didn't seem very interested—but now I recalled my mission.

"What to do? Maybe I should use Steal on the little punk right in front of Iris and leave him half-naked? …No, that would be bad for Iris's education, showing her something sick like that. But this is a prince we're dealing with. I can't get too rough…"

I was muttering to myself, in bed in the room the prime minister had given me for tonight, when it happened. There was a soft knock on the door and a voice from outside.

"Kazuma, are you there? There's something I'd like to talk about. May I come in?"

It was Megumin. I hadn't locked the door yet, since I wasn't planning on going to sleep for a while, so I just called, "It's open!"

"I'm sorry. I know it's late…," Megumin said quietly as she came in, her cheeks a faint red. I wondered what she could want. Was she here to thank me for what I'd done for Iris? Yeah, the two of them seemed to be up to something on the sly. This would be the perfect opportunity to quiz her about it.

…But just as I was thinking that:

"Ahem, may I sit next to you?" Megumin asked, and then without waiting for an answer, she came and seated herself on the bed. Geez, she was sitting awfully close to me.

…Then it hit me. I remembered something from before. What had I said to Megumin? I think it was: *"If you ever feel like you're finally free of the bad feelings surrounding you and that woman, and you come to me just because you want to be with me, I won't have any reason at all to say no."*

And she'd said: *"Is that so? When that time comes, then, I'll visit your room again."*

My heart rate shot through the roof, but I said as calmly as I could, "S-sure, go ahead. And what brings you here tonight? Can't sleep and looking for someone to play a game with? I think Iris is a better opponent for you, closer to your ski—"

Megumin slid closer to me, cutting me off. Maybe it was excitement that made her eyes look so red; it was obvious from her expression that she wasn't going to get any of my jokes right now.

I swallowed. She said, "I want you to sleep with me tonight. Or… would you…rather…not…?" Her voice got smaller and smaller, her hand squeezing mine gently as she looked away in embarrassment.

At long last, the day had come.

After so much waiting and delay, the moment of my triumph was here.

But calm yourself: The first thing to do was to lock the door, make sure no one could barge in. Then, as the older partner and the guy, take the lead, totally cool and not freaking out at all.

I put my hands on Megumin's shoulders, shifting her gently away from me, then went to lock the door...

"Um, Kazuma? I'm not as, er, big as Darkness. Is that...going to be a problem?"

"No, no! I'm a man who can love big and small equally. Please don't take me for such a small-minded person."

Megumin pulled back a little at my somewhat combative answer. "I—I see. In that case...er, I'm somewhat embarrassed, so perhaps you could avert your eyes?"

"Uh-uh."

"Th-that makes it harder for me," she said, thrown by my immediate answer. "The room is still bright. Please, just a little..."

Fine, I guess all I could do was obediently close my eyes. I at least wanted to lock the door, though. Otherwise, who knew what meddling, moment-spoiling buffoon would show up?

So, still somewhat worried but also full of anticipation, I closed my eyes. And at that instant...

I went unconscious.

"...Could... But you..."

"...No, Dark... I... And you..."

I could hear a man and a woman arguing. I tried to force my pounding head to sort out what had happened...

"?!"

That was when I realized there was a ball gag stuffed in my mouth. What was worse, my hands were securely cuffed, and I had been tied with a rope to keep me from moving. I couldn't toss, couldn't turn, couldn't wriggle my way out, and when I used my skills to help me see in the dark, lo and behold, I was in a goddamn closet.

Not this agaaaaaaaiiiiinnn!

As I struggled in the cramped space, I heard the voices once more.

"B-b-but, Kazuma, we come from such different stations in life—it's not that simple... I mean, of course I'm not saying I hate you or anything! I just think maybe it's a little soon for this kind of thing..."

That was Darkness's voice. But while I was still trying to figure out what she was babbling about, I heard the other voice from outside the closet, and it made my blood run cold.

"Forget social station! I throw away my social standing and swear to love you and you alone, Darkness. So come on, let's—!"

It was my voice.

"You throw away your social standing? What would that even mean for a commoner?"

"Huh? Wh-what?"

That dumb stuttering was definitely my voice; I knew it all too well.

"You've been acting a little strange ever since earlier. We're alone together in my room, yet you're so calm and composed. I don't like it."

Damn her. I wanted to burst out of this closet and lay her out flat. There was such a thing as overconfidence; she couldn't expect me to be a pushover forever...

...Well, okay, maybe for a while yet.

"N-no, I'm definitely nervous being alone with you, Darkness, y'know? But come here. Look into my eyes—"

There was my voice again. But before it could go anywhere with what it was saying, Darkness interrupted.

"...Hey, you haven't looked at my chest once since you came in here. What's with that? I can't imagine that, in these circumstances... You aren't the real Kazuma at all, are you?!"

"Hrk!"

I was really starting to worry about what exactly Darkness thought of me. I didn't know quite what was going on out there, but I surmised it was some kind of doppelgänger using my voice. I wasn't sure whether to be thrilled that she knew enough to see through it or enraged that she would say such awful things about me behind my back.

"Now we've come too far. I'll just have to overpower you! This may be his room, but have you noticed he's not around? And if you resist me now, I can't promise he ever will be again…!"

Crap, things were going south in a hurry here. Knowing Darkness's pride and her love for her friends, I was sure she would…

"Wha…! You monster, taking hostages is no fair! Wh-what do you plan to do to me with those handcuffs and that rope? Tie me up?! Do you mean to handcuff me, then tie me up, and then do the most awful things to me?!"

"I don't particularly intend to do anything awful to you; I'll stop at tying you up… G-geez, you're making this unusually easy."

"Hrk—it doesn't matter what happens to me, but leave my friends out of this! Oh, these handcuffs are so cold…! Hey, you, keep using that voice and say, 'Heh-heh, that's a good look on you, Darkness! You know what happens next, don't you?' Give it a touch of arrogance."

"Why, you… A-ahhh, forget it. Here, rope's next, so stop squirming! Hey, I'm not doing anything *weird* to you, so quit blushing!"

"It's just, you're doing *this*, with *that* face…! Hey, what do you plan to do with me? You're not going to stuff me in that cramped, dark closet, and then…!"

I could hear her voice getting louder, and then the closet door opened.

Darkness and I found ourselves eye to eye.

"…Let me guess. You heard the whole thing?"

I nodded.

So there I was in the closet with Darkness, a gag in her mouth and a blush of shame on her face, the two of us looking at the handsome guy in front of us.

"Now then, allow me to enlighten you as to who I am and why I'm doing this." He loomed over us, looking just like me if I were cool as a cucumber, apparently bent on monologizing even though he could have easily kept his mouth shut.

My face, which is to say his face, started to melt until only a dark, humanoid silhouette remained.

"My name is Lugkraft, the doppelgänger. Chief of the Intelligence Bureau of the Demon King's army. And let me tell you, you've put me through the wringer."

The monster with the prime minister's name had a featureless blob of a face, no eyes, or nose, or mouth. But he began to talk to us, despite the fact that we hadn't asked him for any exposition.

"It was more than thirty years ago now. I was finally accepted into Elroad's civil service after many, many attempts, and then I spent every day working like a dog. My colleagues were happier at the casino than the office. The royal family was mad for gambling and so were the nobility. You have no idea how I toiled, with them divesting their assets at the gaming tables day after day… There were times when I thought it would do more for the Demon King's cause merely to leave this country to its own devices."

I thought he was going to brag, but it turned out to be a sob story. Normally, this was where the villain would share his evil plot with the captured hero right before sending him to his doom. But apparently, this guy just had some things he wanted to get off his chest.

Lugkraft, with his tendency to work instead of gamble, quickly gained the trust of the royal family. That was all according to plan. But once he was given a high office and near-complete control of the country's politics, he realized the state the nation was really in. Elroad was collapsing under a pile of debt. The royals and the nobles were willfully ignoring it, just gambling away each day.

"Do you see? These people had gambled away the fortune amassed by their first king at games of chance and had brought the country to the brink of ruin. And how did they come back from the precipice?"

I guess Lugkraft loved his job, because he worked really hard at it. He had been sent as a spy, but his inherently diligent nature and overachieving streak led to a meteoric rise through the ranks. At last, he forgot he had ever been a double agent and dedicated himself to the betterment of Elroad. It was only when he arrived at prime minister, the highest post in the land, that it occurred to him.

"I realized that maybe I hadn't needed to do quite so much work."

I see. He's not diligent; he's just stupid.

"Having become prime minister, I finally went into action. Yes: The moment had come for me to work on behalf of the Demon King. I'm aware you've been spreading rather salacious rumors about him, but the truth is that he's a fine, upstanding individual whom I'm proud to serve…"

This tale of woe and work and pride went on for a while longer until Lugkraft finally gave a contented sigh. "Phew. I've wanted to unburden myself about all these frustrations for so long. I thank you for listening to me."

So he *was* just complaining.

"Ahem, now then, I've been considering how best to take my revenge on you lot, who have reduced all my decades of effort to nothing. At first, I was seized by an almost irresistible desire to kill you, but I forced myself to reconsider."

This sounded like it was going somewhere strange. Darkness, trapped beside me, seemed to have a bad feeling about it, too.

"I thought of the thing you would hate most of all. Namely, for harm to come to your little princess, Iris."

At that, Darkness exclaimed *"Mrrff, mrrf!"* and squirmed violently. But she was tied up so securely, she could hardly move.

"Ah yes, that's the look! That's the look I wanted to see on your face! Ha-ha-ha-ha, I'll just leave you two here. I shall now assume your identities, find your other friends, and tie them up in the same way. And then, once I've told them the same thing I've told you, I'll head to Princess Iris's room!" Lugkraft looked right into my eyes. "I'll have to bear with your pathetic body a while longer. Bwa-ha-ha-ha-ha, yes, that's it! The pain! The suffering!! Fantastic!!"

What a jerk, I thought as he assumed my form and left the room.

6

Darkness and I tried struggling for a while, but we quickly saw that we weren't going to be forcing our way out of this one. Lugkraft had been careful to close the door, too, so no one could hear us in there. Why couldn't our resident moron show up and spoil *this* moment?

Come to think of it, what had Darkness been doing in my room at this hour?

"Mrf! Mrrrf!!"

Whoops. Darkness, the gag still in her mouth, had tried head-butting the door but to no effect. She was on the brink of tears with the thought that her beloved mistress might come to harm, when something in her eyes changed, like she'd had an idea.

Could we roll out of here? Maybe with a little more struggling?

I made eye contact in an attempt to ask these questions, but Darkness didn't seem to understand; she just edged closer, her eyes bloodshot.

"Hrmf, mfff!"

Sorry. I don't know what you're saying.

I tried to communicate that fact to her, but Darkness kept huffing and struggling. Finally, inching forward like a caterpillar, Darkness brought her face closer to mine.

Er…really, really close.

As in, here we were in a crisis, practically cheek to cheek. Heck, she was almost pressed up against me—and look how close our lips were! I had no way to object that this wasn't the time to be doing this; I just had to abandon myself to—

"Hrgh!"

"?!"

She bit down on my ball gag. Despite the gag in her own mouth,

Darkness was trying to use her teeth to pull the one out of mine. I started nodding in time to her movements—toward me, away from me. Until finally...!

"*Kindle*!"

The gag loosened just enough that I was able to utter a single word of magic. The fire spell caught on my gag, setting it alight...!

"Eeeyow-hot-hot-hot!"

The gag eventually crumbled to cinders, but not before scorching my bangs. I wanted to cast Freeze on my forehead, but there was no time for that.

"Darkness, I'm going to use fire magic on you now. If I use Kindle on the ropes that are holding me, it'll take time for them to burn away, and I might not even be able to cut through the scorched ropes. But you..." Darkness nodded vigorously, as if to say she understood already. "*Kindle*!"

I set the ropes holding her on fire.

We ran down the gloomy hallway without so much as a light. Darkness and I tried to navigate the castle, free of our bindings but still handcuffed.

"Okay, Darkness, where's Iris's room?!"

"No idea—it was the prime minister who found places for us. The only room I know about is yours!"

So we didn't know where Aqua and Megumin were staying in this huge castle, either.

I took the opportunity to ask Darkness something that had been bothering me. "Why did you know where I was staying? And what were you doing there so late? I know the prime minister wanted to tie us up so we wouldn't get in his way; did he tell you to come to my room?"

That produced a flinch from Darkness. "A-about that... Look, you did so much for us on this trip, again... This time, I thought maybe I could reward you with something less childish, not just a kiss on the cheek..."

"Perv! I knew you were *Pervi*ness! We're in the middle of a crisis and you were making a booty call! You sick, twisted woman!"

"Y-y-you've got it all wrong! I wasn't going to go that far! I was planning on something a little more soft-core…! And anyway, it meant I was able to save you, so it was for the best, right?!"

I did seem to remember Darkness saying something back at the inn about wanting to thank me properly this time. I wished she had waited until we were back home to do something so important. Not that I was one to talk, seeing as how I had been about to cross the final frontier with Fake Megumin just a few minutes earlier.

"Ahhhhh!"

I knew that voice! An idiot who was willing to point and shout at me, never mind how late it was.

"Now I've found you, you sexual-harassing NEET!"

"So this is where you've been! You are the lowest, the worst, the vilest!"

Aqua and Megumin, in their pajamas, emerged from the darkness.

"'Sexual-harassing NEET'?" That was a new one. What was with these girls? "Hey, don't go around acting like I'm some sort of criminal. I don't have time for your little games! Where's Iris's room? Do you know? This is an emergency. If you know, then spill it."

Aqua and Megumin looked at each other. "Iris's room is just up ahead, but I think you owe us an explanation first. I never imagined, Kazuma, that in the middle of the night, you would sneak into Aqua's room of all places."

I practically exploded at that. "Don't screw with me! I have the right to choose who I want to be with!"

"That's rich, after the way you came into my room and tried to chat me up!" Aqua said. "If Megumin hadn't come by for a visit, I don't know what you might have tried!"

Darkness and I exchanged a quick nod.

"Look, we need to get to Iris's room! And I didn't sneak into Aqua's stupid room! I never touched her, even back when we were sleeping in the stables together! Even at my favorite shop, she's the only one I've never picked!"

"You should be ashamed of yourself! You sounded so passionate! And when I shot you down, suddenly nothing happened? If you *really* wanted to get with me, there are ways, you know—like giving me all your money or bringing gifts of expensive wine! Then I *might* at least let you hold my hand!"

I seriously wanted to smack this dumbass.

Better yet, I wanted to wring Lugkraft's neck for putting me in this position!

"That was a fake me who was talking to you, a doppelgänger! A shape-shifting double has infiltrated this castle! And he's after Iris!"

Aqua and Megumin looked at each other again.

"Hey, so you mean all those nice things you said about my blue hair, that was an imposter talking the whole time? You didn't mean that weird stuff you said about how I would be perfect if only I didn't belong to the Axis Church?"

"And you told me that *I* would be perfect if only I didn't belong to the Crimson Magic Clan, and I won't be satisfied until I've blown you away for that."

They guided us along, all the while saying things I would have been happier not hearing.

Quit it! I don't want to know how that jerk tried to hit on you! Seriously, stop already!

Given his modus operandi, would he actually try to chat up Iris, too? He was convinced she was my little sister, so I didn't really think so, but…!

"This is it! This is Iris's room… Hey, you can hear something from inside."

Crap, he was already in there!

Darkness and I got ready to kick down the door when—!

"*Exterion*!!!"

That happened.

A brutal slash flew directly over my head. An instant later, the door came crashing down, and…

"E-Elder Brother?!"

There stood Iris in her pajamas, blushing furiously. However Lugkraft had tried to get to her, it had caused her to draw her sword—along with a black puddle I assumed was the former prime minister spreading on the floor.

7

"I can't apologize enough!"

The next morning. After everyone learned about the fuss in the castle, we went back to our inn. And then we returned to the castle when it was light again.

"Um, Prince Levy. We know you weren't involved, so please don't…"

The young prince had thrown himself to the ground despite the fact that we were in front of all his retainers, and now Iris was trying to cheer him up. The fact that the prime minister had been a doppelgänger had already spread beyond the castle and was the talk of everyone in town. As for Iris, she wasn't just the Dragonslayer but now also the savior of a country that had nearly been taken over by a shape-shifter.

Any and every citizen of Elroad was aware that this savior was betrothed to their prince, and it had the entire town in a state of celebration.

"I'm sorry! It was all because of my own foolishness. Argh, no wonder they call me the idiot prince! If you hadn't come here, Princess Iris, Elroad would have been subjugated by the Demon King…!"

The prince had been like this for a while now. The news about Lugkraft's identity had been shocking in proportion to how important he had been in this country. Everyone who had previously dismissed Iris as a countrified runt now practically worshipped her, to the point that you almost couldn't be sure who really ran this country anymore.

Now Iris stepped to the center of the audience chamber, smiling at the prostrate prince.

"Your Majesty. Royalty shouldn't be too eager to bow the head, you understand?"

At that, the prince jumped to his feet and coughed loudly. "Y-yes, of course. But we have, I must say, incurred a great debt in this instance. Our nation won't forget what we owe to Belzerg. Ask us for anything you need in future. Ahem…" He hesitated for a second, then went on. "Because Belzerg and Elroad are friends and allies, of course." Then he looked away, embarrassed.

Advisers and Iris alike turned beatific gazes on him, and the whole audience chamber was filled with a sense of harmonious accord.

Darkness, squinting at Iris as if she were too bright to look at, stepped up beside the princess. "Good, now we can consider this matter resolved. All loose ends have been tied up, our friendship has deepened, and the ultimate outcome was positive. We ask for your continued good-will in the future, Prince Levy."

"Indeed. We can only support you from back here, but that we will do to our fullest ability. What a truly fortuitous outcome. I owe a great deal to Princess Iris's elder brother, as well. I can't approve of his tricking me, but that was a valuable lesson in itself." He seemed to be in such high spirits that it felt like our first meeting had been with a different person. "To he who will one day be my own elder brother, I extend a permanent standing invitation to come here anytime and use this castle like his own house."

I didn't really follow. But since nobody seemed like they were going to say anything, I decided to take it on myself to give the prince a word of warning.

"What makes you think I'm going to be your older brother? You must be wrong in the head to get an idea like that."

It was like time in the audience chamber stood still.

"………Er? I'm sorry, but you are Princess Iris's elder brother, aren't you?"

"Sure am. I mean, informally speaking. We don't have a blood connection."

The prince cocked his head. Was it that hard to understand what I'd said?

"No blood connection? What... What are you talking about? Are you not Prince Jatice? But then...who in the world are you?"

"I'm maybe the number one adventurer in all of Belzerg: Kazuma Satou."

Even then, the prince didn't quite seem to be putting the pieces together. "...I see. It's complicated; is that what you're saying? Well, even so, considering Princess Iris reveres you as an older brother, I suppose I, too—"

Maybe he really was an idiot.

"Hold on there. You dissolved your engagement to Iris, remember?"

Now time *really* stopped.

"Hey, hey, you notice he's not moving a muscle? I wonder if he's okay."

"Ahem, I believe we should leave him be. Kazuma, there are certain things you ought not to say. Why would you go out of your way to tell him what everyone else has danced around?"

As Aqua and Megumin whispered to me, the light returned to the prince's eyes.

"A-ahhh, about that... I didn't really mean it! I was just trying to drive a wedge between Belzerg and us so Princess Iris wouldn't want me...! The prime minister had me fooled, too, and it was the ultimate sign of our alliance and friendship...!!"

Now he was downright desperate, the exact opposite of the way he'd been during our first meeting. The prince turned beseeching eyes on Iris. She looked at me, troubled, for only a second.

"...Belzerg and Elroad shall be friends forever and ever. So let us just be friends as well."

"Wait, whaaaaaaat?!"

We watched the capital of Elroad grow smaller in the distance.

"Hey, has it occurred to you that we didn't actually get to enjoy any sightseeing?" Aqua asked from the rearmost seat of the lizard-drawn carriage.

"What, you worry about that *now*? You, the one who has the absolute highest probability of causing a scene anywhere we go?"

"Now just a minute, you night-stalking NEET. If I'd had a little more allowance, I could have had more fun! When we get back to Axel, I want you to raise my allowance! I'll cover one of your turns cooking dinner in exchange…"

Grrr…!

"What did you just say?! 'Night-stalking NEET'?! As if I was even interested in you! Think of all those nights we spent together in the stable! Did I ever do anything to you?!"

"I heard all the fap-fapping from your side of the stable! You were sleeping right next to a gorgeous woman, yeah? Don't try to tell me I wasn't the subject of your little fantasies, you lying NEET!"

What a biiiiiiiitch!

For the first time in a while, my anger reached the boiling point. Despite the fact that the carriage was going full tilt, I worked my way from the driver's bench to where Aqua was seated in the back, bent on reducing her to tears. She must have sensed the danger, because she held up her hands in surrender, but it was too late. Just when I was about to really let her have it, though—

"Ahhh-ha-ha-ha-ha!" Iris, seated next to Megumin, burst into very strange laughter. "Ah-ha-ha-ha-ha ha! Ahhh-ha-ha-ha-ha-ha!"

Completely disarmed by my little princess, I gave up on punishing Aqua and sat down beside her instead. "If you want me to forgive you, you'll do the cooking all this week, right?"

"Sure, but get ready for natto three times a day."

Iris, looking happily at Aqua (who clearly didn't feel the least bit bad), said, "I was right. Every day is wonderful when I'm with you, Elder Brother. I can't thank you enough for taking this quest." She smiled an innocent smile.

"Aw, don't mention it. I had a great time, too. What really shocked me is that you were the only one to see through that fake me. And you haven't even known me as long as anyone else here. What's wrong with the rest of you? How long have we known one another?"

An objection came from the front of the carriage. "Hold it, Kazuma, I saw through him, too! He had me going for a little while there, but then I realized it couldn't be you!"

"You're even worse! The stuff you made him do when he wasn't even me! All he had to do was give you the tiniest push!"

Megumin and Aqua both looked pointedly away.

"As I told Prince Levy, if there's one thing I'm confident in, it's my ability to read people," Iris said, smiling with assurance.

"Hey, Iris, I see your eyes cloud over when you call Kazuma 'Elder Brother'…"

"Sure! You claim to see with unclouded eyes, Aqua, but you couldn't tell me from a monster in disguise. You still think you deserve that nickname? Huh?" While Aqua was busy covering her ears and pretending she couldn't hear me, I remembered something that had slipped my mind all this time. "Oh yeah, Iris, you were so busy with work, you never got to hit the town. It's not much, but I brought you a little souvenir."

It was the kiddie ring I'd bought in town. It cost only four hundred eris, and unfortunately, I'd forgotten to look for anything more expensive. I was a little afraid Iris wouldn't want such a cheap toy, but her eyes opened wide.

"Really? I can have this?"

"Sure. You're missing that ring you always used to wear, right? I can tell—that spot on your finger is kind of white. I thought you might like this one instead."

She took the cheap souvenir, cradling it tenderly with both hands.

"Kazuma, Kazuma, do you have anything like that for me? I think I'm just about the right age to, you know, receive a certain type of ring."

When Megumin predictably butted in, I pulled out the item I had prepared for this very occasion. "Here, Megumin, I've got Elroad rice crackers for you. I don't mind saying they cost more than Iris's ring."

"..............."

Megumin sat with the bag of rice crackers in her hands, a complicated series of emotions playing over her face. I ignored her.

"Oh, Kazumaaaa, what about me? Did you get a souvenir for me?"

"For you, I've got a rock from that gold mine we chased the dragon out of. It's kind of shiny, like maybe it's got some gold in it." I handed her the stone, which might or might not have had any gold in it, and Aqua took it without complaining. She examined it intently. Maybe she liked the shape.

I noticed Darkness shooting furtive glances our way from the driver's bench, but she was driving; I would worry about her later.

Come to think of it, unlike Iris, the girls had all been with me when I went into town. Why was I giving them souvenirs?

But just as I was thinking that…

"Hee… Hee-hee-hee-hee-hee!" Iris, gazing at the ring like it was a genuine treasure, started laughing. "Elder Brother! Er, I mean… Ahem, that is…"

She couldn't quite get the words out. Finally, she braced herself and took a deep breath.

"Thank you, Big Bro."

And then she smiled from ear to ear.

Afterword

Hello from your thankful-that-you-bought-Volume-10, yet-having-been-living-in-Saitama-for-more-than-a-year-has-still-visited-only-the-local-convenience-stores-and-department-store, pretty-much-living-a-*hikikomori*-life author, Natsume Akatsuki. I'm finally living just thirty minutes from Akihabara, but I feel like I hardly go enjoy the city at all.

I'm not especially busy or anything; I've got plenty of time to play games at home. Yet somehow, I feel more like a hermit now than I did when I was living in the mountains.

Knowing what exactly is happening with your author is highly irrelevant, so let's move on to some other present-tense news.

Sneaker Bunko's official website, Sneaker WEB, is currently serializing *An Explosion on This Wonderful World!*

This project sprang from a popularity contest held in conjunction with the premiere of the anime; I was going to do a story about the most popular character(s). It was supposed to be a bonus story of only a few pages, but we got so many votes in the contest that we thought a mere short story would bring down the wrath of our readers, and we promptly changed over to a web serial. The result is a second spin-off featuring Megumin, the winner of the contest, so if you're a fan of things that go boom, check it out.

There's also a whole bunch of manga going on: *Monthly Dragon Age* is serializing the main series and the anthology collections; *Monthly Comic Alive* is running the adaptation of *Explosion!*, and on the web, *Comic Clear* is doing a series of four-panel gag strips. Perhaps you'd like to take a look?

We finally got another little-sister episode this time around, but in the next volume, the problem children will be front and center again. Enjoy!

In this volume, as always, I have to think my illustrator Kurone Mishima-sensei, my editor S-san, the designer, proofreader, marketing people, and everyone else whose help was invaluable in getting this book to print. My heartfelt thanks go out to anyone and everyone who was involved in the production of this volume.

And above all, my deepest thanks to all my readers!

Natsume Akatsuki

AFTERWORD

Iris, resting happily with her new ring.

2016. Kurone Mishima

I'm never leaving this castle again. I've decided to live here forever.

Decided!

That's great, as long as I can live here with you.

YAY!

 You're such selfish babies! Let's go to town and— Huh? Why are there five of us?

 KOMEKKO?! Why are you here? You need to be at home!

Our home went *poof*, and now it's gone!

 ?!?!?!?!

KONOSUBA: GOD'S BLESSING ON THIS WONDERFUL WORLD! 11

COMIN SOON!